Maida's Little Shop

Inez Haynes Irwin

Contents

CHAPTER I: THE RIDE...7

CHAPTER II: CLEANING UP 17

CHAPTER III: THE FIRST DAY 26

CHAPTER IV: THE SECOND DAY 39

CHAPTER V: PRIMROSE COURT 51

CHAPTER VI: TWO CALLS...60

CHAPTER VII: TROUBLE...71

CHAPTER VIII: A RAINY DAY...82

CHAPTER IX: WORK...92

CHAPTER X: PLAY...102

CHAPTER XI: HALLOWEEN 112

CHAPTER XII: THE FIRST SNOW 122

CHAPTER XIII: THE FAIR...130

CHAPTER XIV: CHRISTMAS HAPPENINGS 138

MAIDA'S LITTLE SHOP

BY

Inez Haynes Irwin

CHAPTER I: THE RIDE

Four people sat in the big, shining automobile. Three of them were men. The fourth was a little girl. The little girl's name was Maida Westabrook. The three men were "Buffalo" Westabrook, her father, Dr. Pierce, her physician, and Billy Potter, her friend. They were coming from Marblehead to Boston.

Maida sat in one corner of the back seat gazing dreamily out at the whirling country. She found it very beautiful and very curious. They were going so fast that all the reds and greens and yellows of the autumn trees melted into one variegated band. A moment later they came out on the ocean. And now on the water side were two other streaks of color, one a spongy blue that was sky, another a clear shining blue that was sea. Maida half-shut her eyes and the whole world seemed to flash by in ribbons.

"May I get out for a moment, papa?" she asked suddenly in a thin little voice. "I'd like to watch the waves."

"All right," her father answered briskly. To the chauffeur he said, "Stop here, Henri." To Maida, "Stay as long as you want, Posie."

"Posie" was Mr. Westabrook's pet-name for Maida.

Billy Potter jumped out and helped Maida to the ground. The three men watched her limp to the sea-wall.

She was a child whom you would have noticed anywhere because of her luminous, strangely-quiet, gray eyes and because of the ethereal look given to her face by a floating mass of hair, pale-gold and tendrilly. And yet I think you would have known that she was a sick little girl at the first glance. When she moved, it was with a great slowness as if everything tired her. She was so thin that her hands were like claws and her cheeks scooped in instead of out. She was pale, too, and somehow her eyes looked too big. Perhaps this was because her little heart-shaped face seemed too small.

"You've got to find something that will take up her mind, Jerome," Dr. Pierce said, lowering his voice, "and you've got to be quick about it. Just what Greinschmidt feared has come--that languor--that lack of interest in everything. You've got to find something for her to *do*."

Dr. Pierce spoke seriously. He was a round, short man, just exactly as long any one way as any other. He had springy gray curls all over his head and a nose like a button. Maida thought that he looked like a very old but a very jolly and lovable baby. When he laughed--and he was always laughing with Maida--he shook all over like jelly that has been turned out of a jar. His very curls bobbed. But it seemed to Maida that no matter how hard he chuckled, his eyes were always serious when they rested on her.

Maida was very fond of Dr. Pierce. She had known him all her life. He had gone to college with her father. He had taken care of her health ever since Dr. Greinschmidt left. Dr. Greinschmidt was the great physician who had come all the way across the ocean from Germany to make Maida well. Before the operation Maida could not walk. Now she could walk easily. Ever since she could remember she had always added to her prayers at night a special request that she might some day be like other little girls. Now she was like other little girls, except that she limped. And yet now that she could do all the things that other little girls did, she no longer cared to do them--not even hopping and skipping, which she had always expected would be the greatest fun in the world. Maida herself thought this very strange.

"But what can I find for her to do?" "Buffalo" Westabrook said.

You could tell from the way he asked this question that he was not accustomed to take advice from other people. Indeed, he did not look it. But he looked his name. You would know at once why the cartoonists always represented him with the head of a buffalo; why, gradually, people had forgotten that his first name was Jerome and referred to him always as "Buffalo" Westabrook.

Like the buffalo, his head was big and powerful and emerged from the midst of a shaggy mane. But it was the way in which it was set on his tremendous shoulders that gave him his nickname. When he spoke to you, he looked as if he were about to charge. And the glance of his eyes, set far back of a huge nose, cut through you like a pair of knives.

It surprised Maida very much when she found that people stood in awe of her father. It had never occurred to her to be afraid of him.

"I've racked my brains to entertain her," "Buffalo" Westabrook went on. "I've bought her every gimcrack that's made for children--her nursery looks like a toy factory. I've bought her prize ponies, prize dogs and prize cats--rabbits, guinea-pigs, dancing mice, talking parrots, marmosets--there's a young menagerie at the place in the Adirondacks. I've had a doll-house and a little theater built for her at Pride's. She has her own carriage, her own automobile, her own railroad car. She can have her own flying-machine if she wants it. I've taken her off on trips. I've taken her to the theater and the circus. I've had all kinds of nurses and governesses and companions, but they've been mostly failures. Granny Flynn's the best of the hired people, but of course Granny's old. I've had other children come to stay with her. Selfish little brutes they all turned out to be! They'd play with her toys and ignore her completely. And this fall I brought her to Boston, hoping her cousins would rouse her. But the Fairfaxes decided suddenly to go abroad this winter. If she'd only express a desire for something, I'd get it for her--if it were one of the moons of Jupiter."

"It isn't anything you can *give* her," Dr. Pierce said impatiently; "you must find something for her to *do*."

"Say, Billy, you're an observant little duck. Can't you tell us what's the matter?" "Buffalo" Westabrook smiled down at the third man of the party.

"The trouble with the child," Billy Potter said promptly, "is that everything she's had has been 'prize.' Not that it's spoiled her at all. Petronilla is as simple as a princess in a fairy-tale."

"Petronilla" was Billy Potter's pet-name for Maida.

"Yes, she's wonderfully simple," Dr. Pierce agreed. "Poor little thing, she's lived in a world of bottles and splints and bandages. She's never had a chance to realize either the value or the worthlessness of things."

"And then," Billy went on, "nobody's ever used an ounce of imagination in entertaining the poor child."

"Imagination!" "Buffalo" Westabrook growled. "What has imagination to do with it?"

Billy grinned.

Next to her father and Granny Flynn, Maida loved Billy Potter better than anybody in the world. He was so little that she could never decide whether he was a boy or a man. His chubby, dimply face was the pinkest she had ever seen. From it twinkled a pair of blue eyes the merriest she had ever seen. And falling continually down into his eyes was a great mass of flaxen hair, the most tousled she had ever seen.

Billy Potter lived in New York. He earned his living by writing for newspapers and magazines. Whenever there was a fuss in Wall Street--and the papers always blamed "Buffalo" Westabrook if this happened--Billy Potter would have a talk with Maida's father. Then he wrote up what Mr. Westabrook said and it was printed somewhere. Men who wrote for the newspapers were always trying to talk with Mr. Westabrook. Few of them ever got the chance. But "Buffalo" Westabrook never refused to talk with Billy Potter. Indeed, the two men were great friends.

"He's one of the few reporters who can turn out a good story and tell it straight as I give it to him," Maida had once heard her father say. Maida knew that Billy could turn out good stories--he had turned out a great many for her.

"What has imagination to do with it?" Mr. Westabrook repeated.

"It would have a great deal to do with it, I fancy," Billy Potter answered, "if somebody would only imagine the right thing."

"Well, imagine it yourself," Mr. Westabrook snarled. "Imagination seems to be the chief stock-in-trade of you newspaper men."

Billy grinned. When Billy smiled, two things happened--one to you and the other to him. Your spirits went up and his eyes seemed to disappear. Maida said that Billy's eyes "skrinkled up." The effect was so comic that she always laughed--not with him but at him.

"All right," Billy agreed pleasantly; "I'll put the greatest creative mind of the century to work on the job."

"You put it to work at once, young man," Dr. Pierce said. "The thing I'm trying to impress on you both is that you can't wait too long."

"Buffalo" Westabrook stirred uneasily. His fierce, blue eyes retreated behind the frown in his thick brows until all you could see were two shining points. He watched Maida closely as she limped back to the car. "What are you thinking of, Posie?" he asked.

"Oh, nothing, father," Maida said, smiling faintly. This was the answer she gave most often to her father's questions. "Is there anything you want, Posie?" he was sure to ask every morning, or, "What would you like me to get you to-day, little daughter?" The answer was invariable, given always in the same soft, thin little voice: "Nothing, father--thank you."

"Where are we now, Jerome?" Dr. Pierce asked suddenly.

Mr. Westabrook looked about him. "Getting towards Revere."

"Let's go home through Charlestown," Dr. Pierce suggested. "How would you like to see the house where I was born, Maida--that old place on Warrington Street I told you about yesterday. I think you'd like it, Pinkwink."

"Pinkwink" was Dr. Pierce's pet-name for Maida.

"Oh, I'd love to see it." A little thrill of pleasure sparkled in Maida's flat tones. "I'd just love to."

Dr. Pierce gave some directions to the chauffeur.

For fifteen minutes or more the men talked business. They had come away from the sea and the streams of yellow and red and green trees. Maida pillowed her head on the cushions and stared fixedly at the passing streets. But her little face wore a dreamy, withdrawn look as if she were seeing something very far away. Whenever "Buffalo" Westabrook's glance shot her way, his thick brows pulled together into the frown that most people dreaded to face.

"Now down the hill and then to the left," Dr. Pierce instructed Henri.

Warrington Street was wide and old-fashioned. Big elms marching in a double file between the fine old houses, met in an arch above their roofs. At intervals along the curbstones were hitching-posts of iron, most of them supporting the head of a horse with a ring in his nose. One, the statue of a negro boy with his arms lifted above his head, seemed to beg the honor of holding the reins. Beside these hitching-posts were rectangular blocks of granite--stepping-stones for horseback riders and carriage folk.

"There, Pinkwink," Dr. Pierce said; "that old house on the corner--stop here, Henri, please--that's where I was brought up. The old swing used to hang from that tree and it was from that big bough stretching over the fence that I fell and broke my arm."

Maida's eyes brightened. "And there's the garret window where the squirrels used to come in," she exclaimed.

"The same!" Dr. Pierce laughed. "You don't forget anything, do you? My goodness me! How small the house looks and how narrow the street has grown! Even the trees aren't as tall as they should be."

Maida stared. The trees looked very high indeed to her. And she thought the street quite wide enough for anybody, the houses very stately.

"Now show me the school," she begged.

"Just a block or two, Henri," Dr. Pierce directed.

The car stopped in front of a low, rambling wooden building with a yard in front.

"That's where you covered the ceiling with spit-balls," Maida asked.

"The same!" Dr. Pierce laughed heartily at the remembrance. It seemed to Maida that she had never seen his curls bob quite so furiously before.

"It's one of the few wooden, primary buildings left in the city," he explained to the two men. "It can't last many years now. It's nothing but a rat-trap but how I shall hate to see it go!"

Opposite the school was a big, wide court. Shaded with beautiful trees--maples beginning to flame, horse-chestnuts a little browned, it was lined with wooden toy houses, set back of fenced-in yards and veiled by climbing vines. Pigeons were flying about, alighting now and then to peck at the ground or to preen their green and purple necks. Boys were spinning tops. Girls were jumping rope. The dust they kicked up had a sweet, earthy smell in Maida's nostrils. As she stared, charmed with the picture, a little girl in a scarlet cape and a scarlet hat came climbing up over one of the fences. Quick, active as a squirrel, she disappeared into the next yard.

"Primrose Court!" Dr. Pierce exclaimed. "Well, well, well!"

"Primrose Court," Maida repeated. "Do primroses grow there?"

"Bless your heart, no," Dr. Pierce laughed; "it was named after a man called Primrose who used to own a great deal of the neighborhood."

But Maida was scarcely listening. "Oh, what a cunning little shop!" she exclaimed. "There, opposite the court. What a perfectly darling little place!"

"Good Lord! that's Connors'," Dr. Pierce explained. "Many a reckless penny I've squandered there, my dear. Connors was the funniest, old, bent, dried-up man. I wonder who keeps it now."

As if in answer to his question, a wrinkled old lady came to the window to take a paper-doll from the dusty display there.

"What are those yellow things in that glass jar?" Maida asked.

"Pickled limes," Dr. Pierce responded promptly. "How I used to love them!"

"Oh, father, buy me a pickled lime," Maida pleaded. "I never had one in my life and I've been crazy to taste one ever since I read 'Little Women.'"

"All right," Mr. Westabrook said. "Let's come in and treat Maida to a pickled lime."

A bell rang discordantly as they opened the door. Its prolonged clangor finally brought the old lady from the room at the back. She looked in surprise at the three men in their automobile coats and at the little lame girl.

Coming in from the bright sunshine, the shop seemed unpleasantly dark to Maida. After a while she saw that its two windows gave it light enough but that it was very confused, cluttery and dusty.

Mr. Westabrook bought four pickled limes and everybody ate--three of them with enjoyment, Billy with many wry faces and a decided, "Stung!" after the first taste.

"I like pickled limes," Maida said after they had started for Boston. "What a funny little place that was! Oh, how I would like to keep a little shop just like it."

Billy Potter started. For a moment it seemed as if he were about to speak. But instead, he stared hard at Maida, falling gradually into a brown study. From time to time he came out of it long enough to look sharply at her. The sparkle had all gone out of her face. She was pale and dream-absorbed again.

Her father studied her with increasing anxiety as they neared the big house on Beacon Street. Dr. Pierce's face was shadowed too.

"Eureka! I've found it!" Billy exclaimed as they swept past the State House. "I've got it, Mr. Westabrook."

"Got what?"

Billy did not answer at once. The automobile had stopped in front of a big red-brick house. Over the beautifully fluted columns that held up the porch hung a brilliant red vine. Lavender-colored glass, here and there in the windows, made purple patches on the lace of the curtains.

"Got what?" Mr. Westabrook repeated impatiently.

"That little job of the imagination that you put me on a few moments ago," Billy answered mysteriously. "In a moment," he added with a significant look at Maida. "You stay too, Dr. Pierce. I want your approval."

The door of the beautiful old house had opened and a man in livery came out to assist Maida. On the threshold stood an old silver-haired woman in a black-silk gown, a white cap and apron, a little black shawl pinned about her shoulders.

"How's my lamb?" she asked tenderly of Maida.

"Oh, pretty well," Maida said dully. "Oh, Granny," she added with a sudden flare of enthusiasm, "I saw the cunningest little shop. I think I'd rather tend shop than do anything else in the world."

Billy Potter smiled all over his pink face. He followed Mr. Westabrook and Dr. Pierce into the drawing-room.

Maida went upstairs with Granny Flynn.

Granny Flynn had come straight to the Westabrook house from the boat that brought her from Ireland years ago. She had come to America in search of a runaway daughter but she had never found her. She had helped to nurse Maida's mother in the illness of which she died and she had always taken such care of Maida herself that Maida loved her dearly. Sometimes when they were alone, Maida would call her "Dame," because, she said, "Granny looks just like the 'Dame' who comes into fairy-tales."

Granny Flynn was very little, very bent, very old. "A t'ousand and noine, sure," she always answered when Maida asked her how old. Her skin had cracked into a hundred wrinkles and her long sharp nose and her short sharp chin almost met. But the wrinkles surrounded a pair of eyes that were a twinkling, youthful blue. And her down-turned nose and up-growing chin could not conceal or mar the lovely sweetness of her smile.

Just before Maida went to bed that night, she was surprised by a visit from her father.

"Posie," he said, sitting down on her bed, "did you really mean it to-day when you said you would like to keep a little shop?"

"Oh, yes, father! I've been thinking it over ever since I came home from our ride this afternoon. A little shop, you know, just like the one we saw to-day."

"Very well, dear, you shall keep a shop. You shall keep that very one. I'm going to buy out the business for you and put you in charge there. I've got to be in New York pretty steadily for the next three months and I've decided that I'll send you and Granny to live in the rooms over the shop. I'll fix the place all up for you, give you plenty of money to stock it and then I expect you to run it and make it pay."

Maida sat up in bed with a vigor that surprised her father. She shook her hands--a gesture that, with her, meant great delight. She laughed. It was the first time in months that a happy note had pealed in her laughter. "Oh, father, dear, how good you are to me! I'm just crazy to try it and I know I can make it pay--if hard work helps."

"All right. That's settled. But listen carefully to what I'm going to say, Posie. I can't have this getting into the papers, you know. To prevent that, you're to play a game while you're working in the shop--just as princesses in fairy-tales had to play games sometimes. You're going *in disguise*. Do you understand?"

"Yes, father, I understand."

"You're to pretend that you belong to Granny Flynn, that you're her grand-child. You won't have to tell any lies about it. When the children in the neighbor-hood hear you call her 'Granny,' they'll simply take it for granted that you're her son's child."

"Or I can pretend I'm poor Granny's lost daughter's little girl," Maida suggested.

"If you wish. Billy Potter's going to stay here in Boston and help you. You're to call on him, Posie, if you get into any snarl. But I hope you'll try to settle all your own difficulties before turning to anybody else. Do you understand?"

"Yes, father. Father, dear, I'm so happy. Does Granny know?"

"Yes."

Maida heaved an ecstatic sigh. "I'm afraid I shan't get to sleep to-night--just thinking of it."

But she did sleep and very hard--the best sleep she had known since her operation. And she dreamed that she opened a shop--a big shop this was--on the top of a huge white cloud. She dreamed that her customers were all little boy and girl angels with floating, golden curls and shining rainbow-colored wings. She dreamed that she sold nothing but cake. She used to cut generous slices from an angel-cake as big as the golden dome of the Boston state house. It was very delicious--all honey and jelly and ice cream on the inside, and all frosting, stuck with candies and nuts and fruits, on the outside.

The people on Warrington Street were surprised to learn in the course of a few days that old Mrs. Murdock had sold out her business in the little corner store. For over a week, the little place was shut up. The school children, pouring into the street twice a day, had to go to Main Street for their candy and lead pencils. For a long time all the curtains were kept down. Something was going on inside, but what, could not be guessed from the outside. Wagons deposited all kinds of things at the door, rolls of paper, tins of paint, furniture, big wooden boxes whose contents nobody could guess. Every day brought more and more workmen and the more there were, the harder they worked. Then, as suddenly as it had begun, all the work stopped.

The next morning when the neighborhood waked up, a freshly-painted sign had taken the place over the door of the dingy old black and white one. The lettering was gilt, the background a skyey blue. It read:

CHAPTER II: CLEANING UP

The next two weeks were the busiest Maida ever knew.

In the first place she must see Mrs. Murdock and talk things over. In the second place, she must examine all the stock that Mrs. Murdock left. In the third place, she must order new stock from the wholesale places. And in the fourth place, the rooms must be made ready for her and Granny to live in. It was hard work, but it was great fun.

First, Mrs. Murdock called, at Billy's request, at his rooms on Mount Vernon Street. Granny and Maida were there to meet her.

Mrs. Murdock was a tall, thin, erect old lady. Her bright black eyes were piercing enough, but it seemed to Maida that the round-glassed spectacles, through which she examined them all, were even more so.

"I've made out a list of things for the shop that I'm all out of," she began briskly. "You'll know what the rest is from what's left on the shelves. Now about buying-- there's a wagon comes round once a month and I've told them to keep right on a- coming even though I ain't there. They'll sell you your candy, pickles, pickled limes and all sich stuff. You'll have to buy your toys in Boston--your paper, pens, pencils, rubbers and the like also, but not at the same places where you git the toys. I've put all the addresses down on the list. I don't see how you can make any mistakes."

"How long will it take you to get out of the shop?" Billy asked.

Maida knew that Billy enjoyed Mrs. Murdock, for often, when he looked at that lady, his eyes "skrinkled up," although there was not a smile on his face.

"A week is all I need," Mrs. Murdock declared. "If it worn't for other folks who are keeping me waiting, I'd have that hull place fixed as clean as a whistle in two shakes of a lamb's tail. Now I'll put a price on everything, so's you won't be bothered what to charge. There's some things I don't ever git, because folks buy too many of them and it's sich an everlasting bother keeping them in stock. But you're young and spry, and maybe you won't mind jumping about for every Tom, Dick and Harry. But, remember," she added in parting, "don't git expensive things. Folks in that neighborhood ain't got no money to fool away. Git as many things as you can for a cent a-piece. Git some for five and less for ten and nothing for over a quarter. But you must allus callulate to buy some things to lose money on. I mean the truck you put in the window jess to make folks look in. It gits dusty and fly-specked before you know it and there's an end on it. I allus send them to the Home for Little Wanderers at Christmas time."

Early one morning, a week later, a party of three--Granny Flynn, Billy and Maida--walked up Beacon Street and across the common to the subway. Maida had never walked so far in her life. But her father had told her that if she wanted to keep the shop, she must give up her carriage and her automobile. That was not hard. She was willing to give up anything that she owned for the little shop.

They left the car at City Square in Charlestown and walked the rest of the way. It was Saturday, a brilliant morning in a beautiful autumn. All the children in the neighborhood were out playing. Maida looked at each one of them as she passed. They seemed as wonderful as fairy beings to her--for would they not all be her customers soon? And yet, such was her excitement, she could not remember one face after she had passed it. A single picture remained in her mind--a picture of a little girl standing alone in the middle of the court. Black-haired, black-eyed, a vivid spot of color in a scarlet cape and a scarlet hat, the child was scattering bread-crumbs to a flock of pigeons. The pigeons did not seem afraid of her. They flew close to her feet. One even alighted on her shoulder.

"It makes me think of St. Mark's in Venice," Maida said to Billy.

But, little girl--scarlet cape--flocks of doves--St. Mark's, all went out of her head entirely when she unlocked the door of the little shop.

"Oh, oh, oh!" she cried, "how nice and clean it looks!"

The shop seemed even larger than she remembered it. The confused, dusty, cluttery look had gone. But with its dull paint and its blackened ceiling, it still seemed dark and dingy.

Maida ran behind the counter, peeped into the show cases, poked her head into the window, drew out the drawers that lined the wall, pulled covers from the boxes on the shelves. There is no knowing where her investigations would have ended if Billy had not said:

"See here, Miss Curiosity, we can't put in the whole morning on the shop. This is a preliminary tour of investigation. Come and see the rest of it. This way to the living-room!"

The living-room led from the shop--a big square room, empty now, of course. Maida limped over to the window. "Oh, oh, oh!" she cried; "did you ever see such a darling little yard?"

"It surely is little," Billy agreed, "not much bigger than a pocket handkerchief, is it?"

And yet, scrap of a place as the yard was, it had an air of completeness, a pretty quaintness. Two tiny brick walks curved from the door to the gate. On either side of these spread out microscopic flower-beds, crowded tight with plants. Late-blooming dahlias and asters made spots of starry color in the green. A vine, running over the door to the second story, waved like a crimson banner dropped from the window.

"The old lady must have been fond of flowers," Billy Potter said. He squinted his near-sighted blue eyes and studied the bunches of green. "Syringa bush in one corner. Lilac bush in the other. Nasturtiums at the edges. Morning-glories running up the fence. Sunflowers in between. My, won't it be fun to see them all racing up in the spring!"

Maida jumped up and down at the thought. She could not jump like other children. Indeed, this was the first time that she had ever tried. It was as if her feet were like flat-irons. Granny Flynn turned quickly away and Billy bit his lips.

"I know just how I'm going to fix this room up for you, Petronilla," Billy said, nodding his head mysteriously. "Now let's go into the kitchen."

The kitchen led from the living-room. Billy exclaimed when he saw it and Maida shook her hands, but it was Granny who actually screamed with delight.

Much bigger than the living-room, it had four windows with sunshine pouring in through every one of them. But it was not the four windows nor yet the sunshine that made the sensation--it was the stone floor.

"We'll put a carpet on it if you think it's too cold, Granny," Billy suggested immediately.

"Oh, lave it be, Misther Billy," Granny begged. "'Tis loike me ould home in

Oireland. Sure 'tis homesick Oi am this very minut looking at ut."

"All right," Billy agreed cheerfully. "What you say goes, Granny. Now upstairs to the sleeping-rooms."

To get to the second floor they climbed a little stairway not more than three feet wide, with steps very high, most of them triangular in shape because the stairway had to turn so often. And upstairs--after they got there--consisted of three rooms, two big and square and light, and one smaller and darker.

"The small room is to be made into a bathroom," Billy explained, "and these two big ones are to be your bedrooms. Which one will you have, Maida?"

Maida examined both rooms carefully. "Well, I don't care for myself which I have," she said. "But it does seem as if there were a teeny-weeny more sun in this one. I think Granny ought to have it, for she loves the sunshine on her old bones. You know, Billy, Granny and I have the greatest fun about our bones. Hers are all wrong because they're so old, and mine are all wrong because they're so young."

"All right," Billy agreed. "Sunshiny one for Granny, shady one for you. That's settled! I hope you realize, Miss Maida, Elizabeth, Fairfax, Petronilla, Pinkwink, Posie Westabrook what perfectly bully rooms these are! They're as old as Noah."

"I'm glad they're old," Maida said. "But of course they must be. This house was here when Dr. Pierce was a little boy. And that must have been a long, long, long time ago."

"Just look at the floors," Billy went on admiringly. "See how uneven they are. You'll have to walk straight here, Petronilla, to keep from falling down. That old wooden wainscoting is simply charming. That's a nice old fireplace too. And these old doors are perfect."

Granny Flynn was working the latch of one of the old doors with her wrinkled hands. "Manny's the toime Oi've snibbed a latch loike that in Oireland," she said, and she smiled so hard that her very wrinkles seemed to twinkle.

"And look at the windows, Granny," Billy said. "Sixteen panes of glass each. I hope you'll make Petronilla wash them."

"Oh, Granny, will you let me wash the windows?" Maida asked ecstatically.

"When you're grand and sthrong," Granny promised.

"I know just how I'll furnish the room," Billy said half to himself.

"Oh, Billy, tell me!" Maida begged.

"Can't," he protested mischievously. "You've got to wait till it's all finished before you see hide or hair of it."

"I know I'll die of curiosity," Maida protested. "But then of course I shall be very busy with my own business."

"Ah, yes," Billy replied. "Now that you've embarked on a mercantile career, Miss Westabrook, I think you'll find that you'll have less and less time for the decorative side of life."

Billy spoke so seriously that most little girls would have been awed by his manner. But Maida recognized the tone that he always employed when he was joking her. Beside, his eyes were all "skrinkled up." She did not quite understand what the joke was, but she smiled back at him.

"Now can we look at the things downstairs?" she pleaded.

"Yes," Billy assented. "To-day is a very important day. Behind locked doors and sealed windows, we're going to take account of stock."

Granny Flynn remained in the bedrooms to make all kinds of mysterious measurements, to open and shut doors, to examine closets, to try window-sashes, even to poke her head up the chimney.

Downstairs, Billy and Maida opened boxes and boxes and boxes and drawers and drawers and drawers. Every one of these had been carefully gone over by the conscientious Mrs. Murdock. Two boxes bulged with toys, too broken or soiled to be of any use. These they threw into the ash-barrel at once. What was left they dumped on the floor. Maida and Billy sat down beside the heap and examined the things, one by one. Maida had never seen such toys in her life--so cheap and yet so amusing.

It was hard work to keep to business with such enchanting temptation to play all about them. Billy insisted on spinning every top--he got five going at once--on blowing every balloon--he produced such dreadful wails of agony that Granny came running downstairs in great alarm--on jumping with every jump-rope--the short ones tripped him up and once he sprawled headlong--on playing jackstones--Maida beat him easily at this--on playing marbles--with a piece of crayon he drew a ring on the floor--on looking through all the books--he declared that he was going to buy some little penny-pamphlet fairy-tales as soon as he could save the money. But in spite of all this fooling, they really accomplished a great deal.

They found very few eatables--candy, fruit, or the like. Mrs. Murdock had wisely sold out this perishable stock. One glass jar, however, was crammed full of what Billy recognized to be "bulls-eyes"--round lumps of candy as big as plums and as hard as stones. Billy said that he loved bulls-eyes better than terrapin or broiled live lobster, that he had not tasted one since he was "half-past ten." For the rest of the day, one of his cheeks stuck out as if he had the toothache.

They came across all kinds of odds and ends--lead pencils, blank-books, an old slate pencil wrapped in gold paper which Billy insisted on using to draw pictures on a slate--he made this squeak so that Maida clapped her hands over her ears. They found single pieces from sets of miniature furniture, a great many dolls, rag-dolls, china dolls, celluloid dolls, the latest bisque beauties, and two old-fashioned waxen darlings whose features had all run together from being left in too great a heat.

They went through all these things, sorting them into heaps which they afterwards placed in boxes. At noon, Billy went out and bought lunch. Still squatting on the floor, the three of them ate sandwiches and drank milk. Granny said that Maida had never eaten so much at one meal.

All this happened on Saturday. Maida did not see the little shop again until it was finished.

By Monday the place was as busy as a beehive. Men were putting in a furnace, putting in a telephone, putting in a bathroom, whitening the plaster, painting the woodwork.

Finally came two days of waiting for the paint to dry. "Will it ever, *ever*, EVER dry?" Maida used to ask Billy in the most despairing of voices.

By Thursday, the rooms were ready for their second coat of paint.

"Oh, Billy, do tell me what color it is--I can't wait to see it," Maida begged.

But, "Sky-blue-pink" was all she got from Billy.

Saturday the furniture came.

In the meantime, Maida had been going to all the principal wholesale places in Boston picking out new stock. Granny Flynn accompanied her or stayed at home, according to the way she felt, but Billy never missed a trip.

Maida enjoyed this tremendously, although often she had to go to bed before dark. She said it was the responsibility that tired her.

To Maida, these big wholesale places seemed like the storehouses of Santa Claus.

In reality they were great halls, lined with parallel rows of counters. The counters were covered with boxes and the boxes were filled with toys. Along the aisles between the counters moved crowds of buyers, busily examining the display.

It was particularly hard for Maida to choose, because she was limited by price. She kept recalling Mrs. Murdock's advice, "Get as many things as you can for a cent a-piece." The expensive toys tempted her, but although she often stopped and looked them wistfully over, she always ended by going to the cheaper counters.

"You ought to be thinking how you'll decorate the windows for your first day's sale," Billy advised her. "You must make it look as tempting as possible. I think, myself, it's always a good plan to display the toys that go with the season."

Maida thought of this a great deal after she went to bed at night. By the end of the week, she could see in imagination just how her windows were going to look.

Saturday night, Billy told her that everything was ready, that she should see the completed house Monday morning. It seemed to Maida that the Sunday coming in between was the longest day that she had ever known.

When she unlocked the door to the shop, the next morning, she let out a little squeal of joy. "Oh, I would never know it," she declared. "How much bigger it looks, and lighter and prettier!"

Indeed, you would never have known the place yourself. The ceiling had been whitened. The faded drab woodwork had been painted white. The walls had been colored a beautiful soft yellow. Back of the counter a series of shelves, glassed in by sliding doors, ran the whole length of the wall and nearly to the ceiling. Behind the show case stood a comfortable, cushioned swivel-chair.

"The stuff you've been buying, Petronilla," Billy said, pointing to a big pile of boxes in the corner. "Now, while Granny and I are putting some last touches to the rooms upstairs, you might be arranging the window."

"That's just what I planned to do," Maida said, bubbling with importance. "But you promise not to interrupt me till it's all done."

"All right," Billy agreed, smiling peculiarly. He continued to smile as he opened the boxes.

It did not occur to Maida to ask them what they were going to do upstairs. It did not occur to her even to go up there. From time to time, she heard Granny and Billy laughing. "One of Billy's jokes," she said to herself. Once she thought she heard the chirp of a bird, but she would not leave her work to find out what it was.

When the twelve o'clock whistle blew, she called to Granny and to Billy to come to see the results of her morning's labor.

"I say!" Billy emitted a long loud whistle.

"Oh, do you like it?" Maida asked anxiously.

"It's a grand piece of work, Petronilla," Billy said heartily.

The window certainly struck the key-note of the season. Tops of all sizes and colors were arranged in pretty patterns in the middle. Marbles of all kinds from the ten-for-a-cent "peeweezers" up to the most beautiful, colored "agates" were displayed at the sides. Jump-ropes of variegated colors with handles, brilliantly painted, were festooned at the back. One of the window shelves had been furnished like a tiny room. A whole family of dolls sat about on the tiny sofas and chairs. On the other shelf lay neat piles of blank-books and paper-blocks, with files of pens, pencils, and rubbers arranged in a decorative pattern surrounding them all.

In the show case, fresh candies had been laid out carefully on saucers and platters of glass. On the counter was a big, flowered bowl.

"To-morrow, I'm going to fill that bowl with asters," Maida explained.

"OI'm sure the choild has done foine," Granny Flynn said, "Oi cudn't have done betther mesilf."

"Now come and look at your rooms, Petronilla," Billy begged, his eyes dancing.

Maida opened the door leading into the living-room. Then she squealed her delight, not once, but continuously, like a very happy little pig.

The room was as changed as if some good fairy had waved a magic wand there. All the woodwork had turned a glistening white. The wall paper blossomed with garlands of red roses, tied with snoods of red ribbons. At each of the three windows waved sash curtains of a snowy muslin. At each of the three sashes hung a golden cage with a pair of golden canaries in it. Along each of the three sills marched pots of brilliantly-blooming scarlet geraniums. A fire spluttered and sparkled in the fireplace, and drawn up in front of it was a big easy chair for Granny, and a small easy one for Maida. Familiar things lay about, too. In one corner gleamed the cheerful face of the tall old clock which marked the hours with so silvery a voice and the moon-changes by such pretty pictures. In another corner shone the polished surface of a spidery-legged little spinet. Maida loved both these things almost as much as if they had been human beings, for her mother and her grandmother and her great-grandmother had loved them before her. Needed things caught her eyes everywhere. Here was a little bookcase with all her favorite books. There was a desk, stocked with business-like-looking blank-books. Even the familiar table with Granny's "Book of Saints" stood near the easy chair. Granny's spectacles lay on an open page, familiarly marking the place.

In the center of the room stood a table set for three.

"It's just the dearest place," Maida said. "Billy, you've remembered everything. I thought I heard a bird peep once, but I was too busy to think about it."

"Want to go upstairs?" Billy asked.

"I'd forgotten all about bedrooms." Maida flew up the stairs as if she had never known a crutch.

The two bedrooms were very simple, all white--woodwork, furniture, beds, even the fur rugs on the floor. But they were wonderfully gay from the beautiful paper that Billy had selected. In Granny's room, the walls imitated a flowered chintz. But in Maida's room every panel was different. And they all helped to tell the same happy story of a day's hunting in the time when men wore long feathered hats on their curls, when ladies dressed like pictures and all carried falcons on their wrists.

"Granny, Granny," Maida called down to them, "Did you ever see any place in all your life that felt so *homey*?"

"I guess it will do," Billy said in an undertone.

That night, for the first time, Maida slept in the room over the little shop.

CHAPTER III: THE FIRST DAY

If you had gone into the little shop the next day, you would have seen a very pretty picture.

First of all, I think you would have noticed the little girl who sat behind the counter--a little girl in a simple blue-serge dress and a fresh white "tire"--a little girl with shining excited eyes and masses of pale-gold hair, clinging in tendrilly rings about a thin, heart-shaped face--a little girl who kept saying as she turned round and round in her swivel-chair:

"Oh, Granny, do you think *anybody's* going to buy *anything* to-day?"

Next I think you would have noticed an old woman who kept coming to the living-room door--an old woman in a black gown and a white apron so stiffly starched that it rattled when it touched anything--an old woman with twinkling blue eyes and hair, enclosing, as in a silver frame, a little carved nut of a face--an old woman who kept soothing the little girl with a cheery:

"Now joost you be patient, my lamb, sure somebody'll be here soon."

The shop was unchanged since yesterday, except for a big bowl of asters, red, white and blue.

"Three cheers for the red, white and blue," Maida sang when she arranged them. She had been singing at intervals ever since. Suddenly the latch slipped. The bell rang.

Maida jumped. Then she sat so still in her high chair that you would have thought she had turned to stone. But her eyes, glued to the moving door, had a look as if she did not know what to expect.

The door swung wide. A young man entered. It was Billy Potter.

He walked over to the show case, his hat in his hand. And all the time he looked Maida straight in the eye. But you would have thought he had never seen her before.

"Please, mum," he asked humbly, "do you sell fairy-tales here?"

Maida saw at once that it was one of Billy's games. She had to bite her lips to keep from laughing. "Yes," she said, when she had made her mouth quite firm. "How much do you want to pay for them?"

"Not more than a penny each, mum," he replied.

Maida took out of a drawer the pamphlet-tales that Billy had liked so much.

"Are these what you want?" she asked. But before he could answer, she added in a condescending tone, "Do you know how to read, little boy?"

Billy's face twitched suddenly and his eyes "skrinkled up." Maida saw with a mischievous delight that he, in his turn, was trying to keep the laughter back.

"Yes, mum," he said, making his face quite serious again. "My teacher says I'm the best reader in the room."

He took up the little books and looked them over. "'The Three Boars'-- no,'Bears,'" he corrected himself. "'Puss-in-Boats'--no, 'Boots'; 'Jack-and-the-Bean-Scalp'--no,'Stalk'; 'Jack the Joint-Cooler'--no, 'Giant-Killer'; 'Cinderella,' 'Blue-bird'--no, 'Bluebeard'; 'Little Toody-Goo-Shoes'--no, 'Little Goody-Two-Shoes'; 'Tom Thumb,' 'The Sweeping Beauty,'--no, 'The Sleeping Beauty,' 'The Babes in the Wood.' I guess I'll take these ten, mum."

He felt in all his pockets, one after another. After a long time, he brought out some pennies, "One, two, three, four, five, six, seven, eight, nine, ten," he counted slowly.

He took the books, turned and left the shop. Maida watched him in astonishment. Was he really going for good?

In a few minutes the little bell tinkled a second time and there stood Billy again.

"Good morning, Petronilla," he said pleasantly, as if he had not seen her before that morning, "How's business?"

"Fine!" Maida responded promptly. "I've just sold ten fairy books to the funniest little boy you ever saw."

"My stars and garters!" Billy exclaimed. "Business surely is brisk. Keep that up and you can afford to have a cat. I've brought you something."

He opened the bag he carried and took a box out from it. "Hold out your two hands,--it's heavy," he warned.

In spite of his preparation, the box nearly fell to the floor--it was so much heavier than Maida expected. "What can be in it?" she cried excitedly. She pulled the cover off--then murmured a little "oh!" of delight.

The box was full--cram-jam full--of pennies; pennies so new that they looked like gold--pennies so many that they looked like a fortune.

"Gracious, what pretty money!" Maida exclaimed. "There must be a million here."

"Five hundred," Billy corrected her.

He put some tiny cylindrical rolls of paper on the counter. Maida handled them curiously--they, too, were heavy.

"Open them," Billy commanded.

Maida pulled the papers away from the tops. Bright new dimes fell out of one, bright new nickels came from the other.

"Oh, I'm so glad to have nice clean money," Maida said in a satisfied tone. She emptied the money drawer and filled its pockets with the shining coins. "It was very kind of you to think of it, Billy. I know it will please the children." The thought made her eyes sparkle.

The bell rang again. Billy went out to talk with Granny, leaving Maida alone to cope with her first strange customer.

Again her heart began to jump into her throat. Her mouth felt dry on the inside. She watched the door, fascinated.

On the threshold two little girls were standing. They were exactly of the same size, they were dressed in exactly the same way, their faces were as alike as two peas in a pod. Maida saw at once that they were twins. They had little round, chubby bodies, bulging out of red sweaters; little round, chubby faces, emerging from tall, peaky, red-worsted caps. They had big round eyes as expressionless as glass beads and big round golden curls as stiff as candles. They stared so hard at Maida that she began to wonder nervously if her face were dirty.

"Come in, little girls," she called.

The little girls pattered over to the show case and looked in. But their big round eyes, instead of examining the candy, kept peering up through the glass top at Maida. And Maida kept peering down through it at them.

"I want to buy some candy for a cent," one of them whispered in a timid little voice.

"I want to buy some candy for a cent, too," the other whispered in a voice, even more timid.

"All the cent candy is in this case," Maida explained, smiling.

"What are you going to have, Dorothy?" one of them asked.

"I don't know. What are you going to have, Mabel?" the other answered. They discussed everything in the one-cent case. Always they talked in whispers. And they continued to look more often at Maida than at the candy.

"Have you anything two-for-a-cent?" Mabel whispered finally.

"Oh, yes--all the candy in this corner."

The two little girls studied the corner Maida indicated. For two or three moments they whispered together. At one point, it looked as if they would each buy a long stick of peppermint, at another, a paper of lozenges. But they changed their minds a great many times. And in the end, Dorothy bought two large pickles and Mabel bought two large chocolates. Maida saw them swapping their purchases as they went out.

The two pennies which the twins handed her were still moist from the hot little hands that had held them. Maida dropped them into an empty pocket in the money drawer. She felt as if she wanted to keep her first earnings forever. It seemed to her that she had never seen such *precious-looking* money. The gold eagles which her father had given her at Christmas and on her birthday did not seem half so valuable.

But she did not have much time to think of all this. The bell rang again. This time it was a boy--a big fellow of about fourteen, she guessed, an untidy-looking boy with large, intent black eyes. A mass of black hair, which surely had not been combed, fell about a face that as certainly had not been washed that morning.

"Give me one of those blue tops in the window," he said gruffly. He did not add these words but his manner seemed to say, "And be quick about it!" He threw his money down on the counter so hard that one of the pennies spun off into a corner.

He did not offer to pick the penny up. He did not even apologize. And he looked very carefully at the top Maida handed him as if he expected her to cheat him. Then he walked out.

It was getting towards school-time. Children seemed to spring up everywhere as if they grew out of the ground. The quiet streets began to ring with the cries of boys playing tag, leap frog and prisoners' base. The little girls, much more quiet, squatted in groups on doorsteps or walked slowly up and down, arm-in-arm. But Maida had little time to watch this picture. The bell was ringing every minute now. Once there were six children in the little shop together.

"Do you need any help?" Granny called.

"No, Granny, not yet," Maida answered cheerfully.

But just the same, she did have to hurry. The children asked her for all kinds of things and sometimes she could not remember where she had put them. When in answer to the school bell the long lines began to form at the big doorways, two round red spots were glowing in Maida's cheeks. She drew an involuntary sigh of relief when she realized that she was going to have a chance to rest. But first she counted the money she had taken in. Thirty-seven cents! It seemed a great deal to her.

For an hour or more, nobody entered the shop. Billy left in a little while for Boston. Granny, crooning an old Irish song, busied herself upstairs in her bedroom. Maida sat back in her chair, dreaming happily of her work. Suddenly the bell tinkled, rousing her with a start.

It seemed a long time after the bell rang before the door opened. But at last Maida saw the reason of the delay. The little boy who stood on the threshold was lame. Maida would have known that he was sick even if she had not seen the crutches that held him up, or the iron cage that confined one leg.

His face was as colorless as if it had been made of melted wax. His forehead was lined almost as if he were old. A tired expression in his eyes showed that he did not sleep like other children. He must often suffer, too--his mouth had a drawn look that Maida knew well.

The little boy moved slowly over to the counter. It could hardly be said that he walked. He seemed to swing between his crutches exactly as a pendulum swings in a tall clock. Perhaps he saw the sympathy that ran from Maida's warm heart to her pale face, for before he spoke he smiled. And when he smiled you could not possibly think of him as sick or sad. The corners of his mouth and the corners of his eyes seemed to fly up together. It made your spirits leap just to look at him.

"I'd like a sheet of red tissue paper," he said briskly.

Maida's happy expression changed. It was the first time that anybody had asked her for anything which she did not have.

"I'm afraid I haven't any," she said regretfully.

The boy looked disappointed. He started to go away. Then he turned hopefully. "Mrs. Murdock always kept her tissue paper in that drawer there," he said, pointing.

"Oh, yes, I do remember," Maida exclaimed. She recalled now a few sheets of tissue paper that she had left there, not knowing what to do with them. She pulled the drawer open. There they were, neatly folded, as she had left them.

"What did Mrs. Murdock charge for it?" she inquired.

"A cent a sheet."

Maida thought busily. "I'm selling out all the old stock," she said. "You can have all that's left for a cent if you want it."

"Sure!" the boy exclaimed. "Jiminy crickets! That's a stroke of luck I wasn't expecting."

He spread the half dozen sheets out on the counter and ran through them. He looked up into Maida's face as if he wanted to thank her but did not know how to put it. Instead, he stared about the shop. "Say," he exclaimed, "you've made this store look grand. I'd never know it for the same place. And your sign's a crackajack."

The praise--the first she had had from outside--pleased Maida. It emboldened her to go on with the conversation.

"You don't go to school," she said.

The moment she had spoken, she regretted it. It was plain to be seen, she reproached herself inwardly, why he did not go to school.

"No," the boy said soberly. "I can't go yet. Doc O'Brien says I can go next year, he thinks. I'm wild to go. The other fellows hate school but I love it. I s'pose it's because I can't go that I want to. But, then, I want to learn to read. A fellow can have a good time anywhere if he knows how to read. I can read some," he added in a shamed tone, "but not much. The trouble is I don't have anybody to listen and help with the hard words."

"Oh, let me help you!" Maida cried. "I can read as easy as anything." This was the second thing she regretted saying. For when she came to think of it, she could not see where she was going to have much time to herself.

But the little lame boy shook his head. "Can't," he said decidedly. "You see, I'm busy at home all day long and you'll be busy here. My mother works out and I have to do most of the housework and take care of the baby. Pretty slow work on crutches, you know--although it's easy enough getting round after you get the hang of it. No, I really don't have any time to fool until evenings."

"Evenings!" Maida exclaimed electrically. "Why, that's just the right time! You see I'm pretty busy myself during the daytime--at my business." Her voice grew a little important on that last phrase. "Granny! Granny!" she called.

Granny Flynn appeared in the doorway. Her eyes grew soft with pity when they fell on the little lame boy. "The poor little gossoon!" she murmured.

"Granny," Maida explained, "this little boy can't go to school because his mother works all day and he has to do the housework and take care of the baby, too, and he wants to learn to read because he thinks he won't be half so lonely with books, and you know, Granny, that's perfectly true, for I never suffered half so much with my legs after I learned to read."

It had all poured out in an uninterrupted stream. She had to stop here to get breath.

"Now, Granny, what I want you to do is to let me hear him read evenings until he learns how. You see his mother comes home then and he can leave the baby with her. Oh, do let me do it, Granny! I'm sure I could. And I really think you ought to. For, if you'll excuse me for saying so, Granny, I don't think you can understand as well as I do what a difference it will make." She turned to the boy. "Have you read 'Little Men' and 'Little Women'?"

"No--why, I'm only in the first reader."

"I'll read them to you," Maida said decisively, "and 'Treasure Island' and 'The Princes and the Goblins' and 'The Princess and Curdie.'" She reeled off the long list of her favorites.

In the meantime, Granny was considering the matter. Dr. Pierce had said to her of Maida: "Let her do anything that she wants to do--as long as it doesn't interfere with her eating and sleeping. The main thing to do is to get her ***to want to do things***."

"What's your name, my lad?" she asked.

"Dicky Dore, ma'am," the boy answered respectfully.

"Well, Oi don't see why you shouldn't thry ut, acushla," she said to Maida. "A half an hour iv'ry avening after dinner. Sure, in a wake, 'twill be foine and grand we'll be wid the little store running like a clock."

"We'll begin next week, Monday," Maida said eagerly. "You come over here right after dinner."

"All right." The little lame boy looked very happy but, again, he did not seem to know what to say. "Thank you, ma'am," he brought out finally. "And you, too," turning to Maida.

"My name's Maida."

"Thank you, Maida," the boy said with even a greater display of bashfulness. He settled the crutches under his thin shoulders.

"Oh, don't go, yet," Maida pleaded. "I want to ask you some questions. Tell me the names of those dear little girls--the twins."

Dicky Dore smiled his radiant smile. "Their last name's Clark. Say, ain't they the dead ringers for each other? I can't tell Dorothy from Mabel or Mabel from Dorothy."

"I can't, either," Maida laughed. "It must be fun to be a twin--to have any kind of a sister or brother. Who's that big boy--the one with the hair all hanging down on his face?"

"Oh, that's Arthur Duncan." Dicky's whole face shone. "He's a dandy. He can lick any boy of his size in the neighborhood. I bet he could lick any boy of his size in the world. I bet he could lick his weight in wild-cats."

Maida's brow wrinkled. "I don't like him," she said. "He's not polite."

"Well, I like him," Dicky Dore maintained stoutly. "He's the best friend I've got anywhere. Arthur hasn't any mother, and his father's gone all day. He takes care of himself. He comes over to my place a lot. You'll like him when you know him."

The bell tinkling on his departure did not ring again till noon. But Maida did not mind.

"Granny," she said after Dicky left, "I think I've made a friend. Not a friend somebody's brought to me--but a friend of my very own. Just think of that!"

At twelve, Maida watched the children pour out of the little schoolhouse and disappear in all directions. At two, she watched them reappear from all directions and pour into it again. But between those hours she was so busy that she did not have time to eat her lunch until school began again. After that, she sat undisturbed for an hour.

In the middle of the afternoon, the bell rang with an important-sounding tinkle. Immediately after, the door shut with an important-sounding slam. The footsteps, clattering across the room to the show case, had an important-sounding tap. And the little girl, who looked inquisitively across the counter at Maida, had decidedly an important manner.

She was not a pretty child. Her skin was too pasty, her blue eyes too full and staring. But she had beautiful braids of glossy brown hair that came below her waist. And you would have noticed her at once because of the air with which she wore her clothes and because of a trick of holding her head very high.

Maida could see that she was dressed very much more expensively than the other children in the neighborhood. Her dark, blue coat was elaborate with straps and bright buttons. Her pale-blue beaver hat was covered with pale-blue feathers. She wore a gold ring with a turquoise in it, a silver bracelet with a monogram on it, a little gun-metal watch pinned to her coat with a gun-metal pin, and a long string of blue beads from which dangled a locket.

Maida noticed all this decoration with envy, for she herself was never permitted to wear jewelry. Occasionally, Granny would let her wear one string from a big box of bead necklaces which Maida had bought in Venice.

"How much is that candy?" the girl asked, pointing to one of the trays.

Maida told her.

"Dear me, haven't you anything better than that?"

Maida gave her all her prices.

"I'm afraid there's nothing good enough here," the little girl went on disdainfully. "My mother won't let me eat cheap candy. Generally, she has a box sent over twice a week from Boston. But the one we expected to-day didn't come."

"The little girl likes to make people think that she has nicer things than anybody else," Maida thought. She started to speak. If she had permitted herself to go on, she would have said: "The candy in this shop is quite good enough for any little girl. But I won't sell it to you, anyway." But, instead, she said as quietly as she could:

"No, I don't believe there's anything here that you'll care for. But I'm sure you'll find lots of expensive candy on Main Street."

The little girl evidently was not expecting that answer. She lingered, still looking into the show case. "I guess I'll take five cents' worth of peppermints," she said finally. Some of the importance had gone out of her voice.

Maida put the candy into a bag and handed it to her without speaking. The girl bustled towards the door. Half-way, she stopped and came back.

"My name is Laura Lathrop," she said. "What's yours?"

"Maida."

"Maida?" the girl repeated questioningly. "Maida?--oh, yes, I know--Maida Flynn. Where did you live before you came here?"

"Oh, lots of places."

"But where?" Laura persisted.

"Boston, New York, Newport, Pride's Crossing, the Adirondacks, Europe."

"Oh, my! Have you been to Europe?" Laura's tone was a little incredulous.

"I lived abroad a year."

"Can you speak French?"

"Oui, Mademoiselle, je parle Francais un peu."

"Say some more," Laura demanded.

Maida smiled. "Un, deux, trois, quatre, cinq, six, sept, huit, neuf, dix, onze, douze--"

Laura looked impressed. "Do you speak any other language?"

"Italian and German--a very little."

Laura stared hard at her and her look was full of question. But it was evident that she decided to believe Maida.

"I live in Primrose Court," she said, and now there was not a shadow of condescension left in her voice. "That large house at the back with the big lawn about it. I'd like to have you come and play with me some afternoon. I'm very busy most of the time, though. I take music and fancy dancing and elocution. Next winter, I'm going to take up French. I'll send you word some afternoon when I have time to play."

"Thank you," Maida said in her most civil voice. "Come and play with me sometime," she added after a pause.

"Oh, my mother doesn't let me play in other children's houses," Laura said airily. "Good-bye."

"Good-bye," Maida answered.

She waited until Laura had disappeared into the court. "Granny," she called impetuously, "a little girl's been here who I think is the hatefullest, horridest, disagreeablest thing I ever saw in my life."

"Why, what did the choild do?" Granny asked in surprise.

"Do?" Maida repeated. "She did everything. Why, she--she--" She interrupted herself to think hard a moment. "Well, it's the queerest thing. I can't tell you a thing she did, Granny, and yet, all the time she was here I wanted to slap her."

"There's manny folks that-a-way," said Granny. "The woisest way is to take no notuce av ut."

"Take no notice of it!" Maida stormed. "It's just like not taking any notice of a bee when it's stinging you."

Maida was so angry that she walked into the living-room without limping.

At four that afternoon, when the children came out of school, there was another flurry of trade. Towards five, it slackened. Maida sat in her swivel-chair and wistfully watched the scene in the court. Little boys were playing top. Little girls were jumping rope. Once she saw a little girl in a scarlet cape come out of one of the yards. On one shoulder perched a fluffy kitten. Following her, gamboled an Irish setter and a Skye terrier. Presently it grew dark and the children began to go indoors. Maida lighted the gas and lost herself in "Gulliver's Travels."

The sound of voices attracted her attention after awhile. She turned in her chair. Outside, staring into the window, stood a little boy and girl--a ragged, dirty pair. Their noses pressed so hard against the glass that they were flattened into round white circles. They took no notice of Maida. Dropping her eyes to her book, she pretended to read.

"I boneys that red top, first," said the little boy in a piping voice.

He was a round, brown, pop-eyed, big-mouthed little creature. Maida could not decide which he looked most like--a frog or a brownie. She christened him "the Bogle" at once.

"I boneys that little pink doll with the curly hair, first," said the girl.

She was a round, brown little creature, too--but pretty. She had merry brown eyes and a merry little red and white smile. Maida christened her "the Robin."

"I boneys that big agate, second," said the Bogle.

"I boneys that little table, second," said the Robin.

"I boneys that knife, third," said the Bogle.

"I boneys that little chair, third," said the Robin.

Maida could not imagine what kind of game they were playing. She went to the door. "Come in, children," she called.

The children jumped and started to run away. But they stopped a little way off, turned and stood as if they were not certain what to do. Finally the Robin marched over to Maida's side and the Bogle followed.

"Tell me about the game you were playing," Maida said. "I never heard of it before."

"'Tain't any game," the Bogle said.

"We were just boneying," the Robin explained. "Didn't you ever boney anything?"

"No."

"Why, you boneys things in store windows," the Robin went on. "You always boney with somebody else. You choose one thing for yours and they choose something else for theirs until everything in the window is all chosen up. But of course they don't really belong to you. You only play they do."

"I see," Maida said.

She went to the window and took out the red top and the little pink doll with curly hair. "Here, these are the things you boneyed first. You may have them."

"Oh, thank you--thank you--thank you," the Robin exclaimed. She kissed the little pink doll ecstatically, stopping now and then to look gratefully at Maida.

"Thank you," the Bogle echoed. He did not look at Maida but he began at once to wind his top.

"What is your name?" Maida asked.

"Molly Doyle," the Robin answered. "And this is my brother, Timmie Doyle."

"My name's Maida. Come and see me again, Molly, and you, too, Timmie."

"Of course I'll come," Molly answered, "and I'm going to name my doll 'Maida.'"

Molly ran all the way home, her doll tightly clutched to her breast. But Timmie stopped to spin his top six times--Maida counted.

No more customers came that evening. At six, Maida closed and locked the shop.

After dinner she thought she would read one of her new books. She settled herself in her little easy chair by the fire and opened to a story with a fascinating picture. But the moment her eyes fell on the page--it was the strangest thing--a drowsiness, as deep as a fairy's enchantment, fell upon her. She struggled with it for awhile, but she could not throw it off. The next thing she knew, Granny was helping her up the stairs, was undressing her, had laid her in her bed. The next thing she was saying dreamily, "I made one dollar and eighty-seven cents to-day. If my papa ever gets into any more trouble in Wall Street, he can borrow from me."

The next thing, she felt the pillow soft and cool under her cheek. The next thing--bright sunlight was pouring through the window--it was morning again.

CHAPTER IV: THE SECOND DAY

It had rained all that night, but the second morning dawned the twinklingest kind of day. It seemed to Maida that Mother Nature had washed a million tiny, fleecy, white clouds and hung them out to dry in the crisp blue air. Everything still dripped but the brilliant sunshine put a sparkle on the whole world. Slates of old roofs glistened, brasses of old doors glittered, silver of old name-plates shone. Curbstones, sidewalks, doorsteps glimmered and gleamed. The wet, ebony-black trunks of the maples smoked as if they were afire, their thick-leaved, golden heads flared like burning torches. Maida stood for a long time at the window listening to a parrot who called at intervals from somewhere in the neighborhood. "Get up, you sleepy-heads! Get up! Get up!"

A huge puddle stretched across Primrose Court. When Maida took her place in the swivel-chair, three children had begun already to float shingles across its muddy expanse. Two of them were Molly and Tim Doyle, the third a little girl whom Maida did not know. For a time she watched them, fascinated. But, presently, the school children crowding into the shop took all her attention. After the bell rang and the neighborhood had become quiet again, she resumed her watch of the mud-puddle fun.

Now they were loading their shingles with leaves, twigs, pebbles, anything that they could find in the gutters. By lashing the water into waves, as they trotted in the wake of their frail craft, they managed to sail them from one end of the puddle to the other. Maida followed the progress of these merchant vessels as breathlessly as their owners. Some capsized utterly. Others started to founder and had to be dragged ashore. A few brought the cruise to a triumphant finish.

But Tim soon put an end to this fun. Unexpectedly, his foot caught somewhere and he sprawled headlong in the tide. "Oh, Tim!" Molly said. But she said it without surprise or anger. And Tim lay flat on his stomach without moving, as if it were a common occurrence with him. Molly waded out to him, picked him up and marched him into the house.

The other little girl had disappeared. Suddenly she came out of one of the yards, clasping a Teddy-bear and a whole family of dolls in her fat arms. She sat down at the puddle's edge and began to undress them. Maida idly watched the busy little fingers--one, two, three, four, five--now there were six shivering babies. What was she going to do with them? Maida wondered.

"Granny," Maida called, "do come and see this little girl! She's--" But Maida did not finish that sentence in words. It ended in a scream. For suddenly the little girl threw the Teddy-bear and all the six dolls into the puddle. Maida ran out the door. Half-way across the court she met Dicky Dore swinging through the water. Between them they fished all the dolls out. One was of celluloid and another of rubber--they had floated into the middle of the pond. Two china babies had sunk to the very bottom--their white faces smiled placidly up through the water at their rescuers. A little rag-doll lay close to the shore, water-logged. A pretty paper-doll had melted to a pulp. And the biggest and prettiest of them, a lovely blonde creature with a shapely-jointed body and a bisque head, covered with golden curls, looked hopelessly bedraggled.

"Oh, Betsy Hale!" Dicky said. "You naughty, naughty girl! How could you drown your own children like that?"

"I were divin' them a baff," Betsy explained.

Betsy was a little, round butterball of a girl with great brown eyes all tangled up in eyelashes and a little pink rosebud of a mouth, folded over two rows of mice-teeth. She smiled deliciously up into Maida's face:

"I aren't naughty, is I?" she asked.

"Naughty? You bunny-duck! Of course you are," Maida said, giving her a bear-hug. "I don't see how anybody can scold her," she whispered to Dicky.

"Scold her! You can't," Dicky said disgustedly. "She's too cute. And then if you did scold her it wouldn't do any good. She's the naughtiest baby in the neighbor-hood--although," he added with pride, "I think Delia's going to be pretty nearly as naughty when she gets big enough. But Betsy Hale--why, the whole street has to keep an eye on her. Come, pick up your dollies, Betsy," he wheedled, "they'll get cold if you leave them out here."

The thought of danger to her darlings produced immediate activity on Betsy's part. She gathered the dolls under her cape, hugging them close. "Her must put her dollies to bed," she said wisely.

"Calls herself *her* half the time," Dicky explained. He gathered up the dresses and shooing Betsy ahead of him, followed her into the yard.

"She's the greatest child I ever saw," he said, rejoining Maida a little later. "The things she thinks of to do! Why, the other day, Miss Allison--the sister of the blind lady what sits in the window and knits--the one what owns the parrot--well, Miss Allison painted one of her old chairs red and put it out in the yard to dry. Then she washed a whole lot of lace and put that out to dry. Next thing she knew she looked out and there was Betsy washing all the red paint off the chair with the lace. You'd have thought that would have been enough for one day, wouldn't you? Well, that afternoon she turned the hose on Mr. Flanagan--that's the policeman on the beat."

"What did he say?" Maida asked in alarm. She had a vague imaginary picture of Betsy being dragged to the station-house.

"Roared! But then Mr. Flanagan thinks Betsy's all right. Always calls her 'sophy Sparkles.' Betsy runs away about twice a week. Mr. Flanagan's always finding her and lugging her home. I guess every policeman in Charlestown knows her by this time. There, look at her now! Did you ever see such a kid?"

Betsy had come out of the yard again. She was carrying a huge feather duster over her head as if it were a parasol.

"The darling!" Maida said joyously. "I hope she'll do something naughty every day."

"Queer how you love a naughty child," Dick said musingly. "They're an awful lot of trouble but you can't help liking them. Has Tim Doyle fallen into the puddle yet?"

"Yes, just a little while ago."

"He's always falling in mud puddles. I guess if Molly fishes him out once after a rain, she does a half a dozen times."

"Do come and see me, Dicky, won't you?" Maida asked when they got to the shop door. "You know I shall be lonely when all the children are in school and--then besides--you're the first friend I've made."

At the word ***friend***, Dicky's beautiful smile shone bright. "Sure, I'll come," he said heartily. "I'll come often."

"Granny," Maida exclaimed, bursting into the kitchen, "wait until you hear about Betsy Hale." She told the whole story. "Was I ever a naughty little girl?" she concluded.

"Naughty? Glory be, and what's ailing you? 'Twas the best choild this side of Heaven that you was. Always so sick and yet niver a cross wurrud out of you."

A shadow fell over Maida's face. "Oh, dear, dear," she grieved. "I wish I had been a naughty child--people love naughty children so. Are you quite sure I was always good, Granny?"

"Why, me blessid lamb, 'twas too sick that you was to be naughty. You cud hardly lift one little hand from the bed."

"But, Granny, dear," Maida persisted, "can't you think of one single, naughty thing I did? I'm sure you can if you try hard."

Maida's face was touched with a kind of sad wistfulness. Granny looked down at her, considerably puzzled. Then a light seemed to break in her mind. It shone through her blue eyes and twinkled in her smile.

"Sure and Oi moind wance when Oi was joost afther giving you some medicine and you was that mad for having to take the stuff that you sat oop in bed and knocked iv'ry bottle off the table. Iv'ry wan! Sure, we picked oop glass for a wake afther."

Maida's wistful look vanished in a peal of silvery laughter. "Did I really, Granny?" she asked in delight. "Did I break every bottle? Are you sure? Every one?"

"Iv'ry wan as sure as OI'm a living sinner," said Granny. "Faith and 'twas the bad little gyurl that you was often--now that I sthop to t'ink av ut."

Maida bounded back to the shop in high spirits. Granny heard her say "Every bottle!" again and again in a whispering little voice.

"Just think, Granny," she called after a while. "I've made one, two, three, four, five friends--Dicky, Molly, Tim, Betsy and Laura--though I don't call her quite a friend yet. Pretty good for so soon!"

Maida was to make a sixth friend, although not quite so quickly.

It began that noontime with a strange little scene that acted itself out in front of Maida's window. The children had begun to gather for school, although it was still very quiet. Suddenly around the corner came a wild hullaballoo--the shouts of small boys, the yelp of a dog, the rattle and clang of tin dragged on the brick sidewalk. In another instant appeared a dog, a small, yellow cur, collarless and forlorn-looking, with a string of tin cans tied to his tail, a horde of small boys yelling after him and pelting him with stones.

Maida started up, but before she could get to the door, something flashed like a scarlet comet from across the street. It was the little girl whom Maida had seen twice before--the one who always wore the scarlet cape.

Even in the excitement, Maida noticed how handsome she was. She seemed proud. She carried her slender, erect little body as if she were a princess and her big eyes cast flashing glances about her. Jet-black were her eyes and hair, milk-white were her teeth but in the olive of her cheeks flamed a red such as could be matched only in the deepest roses. Maida christened her Rose-Red at once.

Rose-Red lifted the little dog into her arms with a single swoop of her strong arm. She yanked the cans from its tail with a single indignant jerk. Fondling the trembling creature against her cheek, she talked first to him, then to his abashed persecutors.

"You sweet, little, darling puppy, you! Did they tie the wicked cans to his poor little tail!" and then--"if ever I catch one of you boys treating a poor, helpless animal like this again, I'll shake the breath out of your body--was he the beautifullest dog that ever was? And if that isn't enough, Arthur Duncan will lick you all, won't you, Arthur?" She turned pleadingly to Arthur.

Arthur nodded.

"Nobody's going to hurt helpless creatures while I'm about! He was a sweet little, precious little, pretty little puppy, so he was."

Rose-Red marched into the court with the puppy, opened a gate and dropped him inside.

"That pup belongs to me, now," she said marching back.

The school bell ringing at this moment ended the scene.

"Who's that little girl who wears the scarlet cape?" Maida asked Dorothy and Mabel Clark when they came in together at four.

"Rosie Brine," they answered in chorus.

"She's a dreffle naughty girl," Mabel said in a whisper, and "My mommer won't let me play with her," Dorothy added.

"Why not?" Maida asked.

"She's a tom-boy," Mabel informed her.

"What's a tom-boy?" Maida asked Billy that night at dinner.

"A tom-boy?" Billy repeated. "Why, a tom-boy is a girl who acts like a boy."

"How can a girl be a boy?" Maida queried after a few moments of thought. "Why don't they call her a tom-girl?"

"Why, indeed?" Billy answered, taking up the dictionary.

Certainly Rosie Brine acted like a boy--Maida proved that to herself in the next few days when she watched Rose-Red again and again. But if she were a tom-boy, she was also, Maida decided, the most beautiful and the most wonderful little girl in the world. And, indeed, Rosie was so full of energy that it seemed to spurt out in the continual sparkle of her face and the continual movement of her body. She never walked. She always crossed the street in a series of flying jumps. She never went through a gate if she could go over the fence, never climbed the fence if she could vault it. The scarlet cape was always flashing up trees, over sheds, sometimes to the very roofs of the houses. Her principal diversion seemed to be climbing lamp-posts. Maida watched this proceeding with envy. One athletic leap and Rose-Red was clasping the iron column half-way up--a few more and she was swinging from the bars under the lantern. But she was accomplished in other ways. She could spin tops, play "cat" and "shinney" as well as any of the boys. And as for jumping rope--if two little girls would swing for her, Rosie could actually waltz in the rope.

The strangest thing about Rosie was that she did not always go to school like the other children. The incident of the dog happened on Thursday. Friday morning, when the children filed into the schoolhouse, Rosie did not follow them. Instead, she hid herself in a doorway until after the bell rang. A little later she sneaked out of her hiding place, joined Arthur Duncan at the corner, and disappeared into the distance. Just before twelve they both came back. For a few moments, they kept well concealed on a side street, out of sight of Primrose Court. But, at intervals, Rosie or Arthur would dart out to a spot where, without being seen, they could get a glimpse of the church clock. When the children came out of school at twelve, they joined the crowd and sauntered home.

Monday morning Maida saw them repeat these maneuvers. She was completely mystified by them and yet she had an uncomfortable feeling. They were so stealthy that she could not help guessing that something underhand was going on.

"Do you know Rosie Brine?" Maida asked Dicky Dore one evening when they were reading together.

"Sure!" Dicky's face lighted up. "Isn't she a peach?"

"They say she is a tom-boy," Maida objected. "Is she?"

"Surest thing you know," Dicky said cheerfully. "She won't take a dare. You ought to see her playing stumps. There's nothing a boy can do that she won't do. And have you noticed how she can spin a top--the best I ever saw for a girl."

Then boys liked girls to be tom-boys. This was a great surprise.

"How does it happen that she doesn't go to school often?"

Dicky grinned. "Hooking jack!"

"Hooking jack?" Maida repeated in a puzzled tone.

"Hooking jack--playing hookey--playing truant." Dicky watched Maida's face but her expression was still puzzled. "Pretending to go to school and not going," he said at last.

"Oh," Maida said. "I understand now."

"She just hates school," Dicky went on. "They can't make her go. Old Stoopendale, the truant officer, is always after her. Little she cares for old Stoopy though. She gets fierce beatings for it at home, too. Funny thing about Rosie--she won't tell a lie. And when her mother asks her about it, she always tells the truth. Sometimes her mother will go to the schoolhouse door with her every morning and afternoon for a week. But the moment she stops, Rosie begins to hook jack again."

"Mercy me!" Maida said. In all her short life she had never heard anything like this. She was convinced that Rosie Brine was a very naughty little girl. And yet, underneath this conviction, burned an ardent admiration for her.

"She must be very brave," she said soberly.

"Brave! Well, I guess you'd think so! Arthur Duncan says she's braver than a lot of boys he knows. Arthur and she hook jack together sometimes. And, oh cracky, don't they have the good times! They go down to the Navy Yard and over to the Monument Grounds. Sometimes they go over to Boston Common and the Public Garden. Once they walked all the way to Franklin Park. And in the summer they often walk down to Crescent Beach. They say when I get well, I can go with them."

Dicky spoke in the wistful tone with which he always related the deeds of stronger children. Maida knew exactly how he felt--she had been torn by the same hopes and despairs.

"Oh, wouldn't it be grand to be able to do just anything?" she said. "I'm just beginning to feel as if I could do some of the things I've always wanted to do."

"I'm going to do them all, sometime," Dicky prophesied. "Doc O'Brien says so."

"I think Rosie the beautifullest little girl," Maida said. "I wish she'd come into the shop so that I could get acquainted with her."

"Oh, she'll come in sometime. You see the W.M.N.T. is meeting now and we're all pretty busy. She's the only girl in it."

"The W.M.N.T.," Maida repeated. "What does that mean?"

"I can't tell?" Dicky said regretfully. "It's the name of our club. Rosie and Arthur and I are the only ones who belong."

After that talk, Maida watched Rosie Brine closer than ever. If she caught a glimpse of the scarlet cape in the distance, it was hard to go on working. She noticed that Rosie seemed very fond of all helpless things. She was always wheeling out the babies in the neighborhood, always feeding the doves and carrying her kitten about on her shoulder, always winning the hearts of other people's dogs and then trying to induce them not to follow her.

"It seems strange that she never comes into the shop," Maida said mournfully to Dicky one day.

"You see she never has any money to spend," Dicky explained. "That's the way her mother punishes her. But sometimes she earns it on the sly taking care of babies. She loves babies and babies always love her. Delia'll go to her from my mother any time and as for Betsy Hale--Rosie's the only one who can do anything with her."

But a whole week passed. And then one day, to Maida's great delight, the tinkle of the bell preceded the entrance of Rose-Red.

"Let me look at your tops, please," Rosie said, marching to the counter with the usual proud swing of her body.

Seen closer, she was even prettier than at a distance. Her smooth olive skin glistened like satin. Her lips showed roses even more brilliant than those that bloomed in her cheeks. A frown between her eyebrows gave her face almost a sullen look. But to offset this, her white teeth turned her smile into a flash of light. Maida lifted all the tops from the window and placed them on the counter.

"Mind if I try them?" Rosie asked.

"Oh, do."

Rosie wound one of them with an expert hand. Then with a quick dash forward of her whole arm, she threw the top to the floor. It danced there, humming like a whole hiveful of bees.

"Oh, how lovely!" Maida exclaimed. Then in fervent admiration: "What a wonderful girl you are!"

Rosie smiled. "Easy as pie if you know how. Want to learn?"

"Oh, will you teach me?"

"Sure! Begin now."

Maida limped from behind the counter. Rosie watched her. Rosie's face softened with the same pity that had shone on the frightened little dog.

"She's sorry for me," Maida thought. "How sweet she looks!"

But Rosie said nothing about Maida's limp. She explained the process of top-spinning from end to end, step by step, making Maida copy everything that she did. At first Maida was too eager--her hands actually trembled. But gradually she gained in confidence. At last she succeeded in making one top spin feebly.

"Now you've got the hang of it," Rosie encouraged her, "You'll soon learn. All you want to do is to practice. I'll come to-morrow and see how you're getting on."

"Oh, do," Maida begged, "and come to see me in the evening sometime. Come this evening if your mother'll let you."

Rosie laughed scornfully. "I guess nobody's got anything to say about *letting me*, if I make up my mind to come. Well, goodbye!"

She whirled out of the shop and soon the scarlet cape was a brilliant spot in the distance.

But about seven that evening the bell rang. When Maida opened the door there stood Rosie.

"Oh, Rosie," Maida said joyfully, throwing her arms about her guest, "how glad I am to see you!" She hurried her into the living-room where Billy Potter was talking with Granny. "This is Rosie Brine, Billy," she said, her voice full of pride in her new friend. "And this is Billy Potter, Rosie."

Billy shook hands gravely with the little girl. And Rosie looked at him in open wonder. Maida knew exactly what she was thinking. Rosie was trying to make up her mind whether he was a boy or a man. The problem seemed to grow more perplexing as the evening went on. For part of the time Billy played with them, sitting on the floor like a boy, and part of the time he talked with Granny, sitting in a chair like a man.

Maida showed Rosie her books, her Venetian beads, all her cherished possessions. Rosie liked the canaries better than anything. "Just think of having six!" she said. Then, sitting upstairs in Maida's bedroom, the two little girls had a long confidential talk.

"I've been just crazy to know you, Maida," Rosie confessed. "But there was no way of getting acquainted, for you always stayed in the store. I had to wait until I could tease mother to buy me a top."

"That's funny," Maida said, "for I was just wild to know you. I kept hoping that you'd come in. I hope you'll come often, Rosie, for I don't know any other little girl of my own age."

"You know Laura Lathrop, don't you?" Rosie asked with a sideways look.

"Yes, but I don't like her."

"Nobody likes her," Rosie said. "She's too much of a smarty-cat. She loves to get people over there and then show off before them. And then she puts on so many airs. I won't have anything to do with her."

From the open window came the shrill scream of Miss Allison's parrot. "What do you think of that?" it called over and over again.

"Isn't that a clever bird?" Rosie asked admiringly. "His name is Tony. I have lots of fun with him. Did you ever see a parrot that could talk, before?"

"Oh, yes, we have several at Pride's."

"Pride's?"

"Pride's Crossing. That's where we go summers."

"And what do your parrots say?"

"One talked in French. He used to say 'Taisez-vous' so much that sometimes we would have to put a cover over the cage to stop him."

"And did you have other animals besides parrots?" Rosie asked. "I love animals."

"Oh, yes, we had horses and dogs and cats and rabbits and dancing mice and marmosets and macaws and parokets and--I guess I've forgotten some of them. But if you like animals, you ought to go to our place in the Adirondacks--there are deer preserves there and pheasants and peacocks."

"Who do they belong to?"

"My father."

Rosie considered this. "Does he keep a bird-place?" she asked in a puzzled tone.

"No." Maida's tone was a little puzzled too. She did not know what a bird-place was.

"Well, did he sell them?"

"I don't think he ever sold any. He gave a great many away, though."

When Rosie went home, Maida walked as far as her gate with her.

"Want to know a secret, Maida?" Rosie asked suddenly, her eyes dancing with mischief.

"Oh, yes. I love secrets."

"Cross your throat then."

Maida did not know how to cross her throat but Rosie taught her.

"Well, then," Rosie whispered, "my mother doesn't know that I went to your house. She sent me to bed for being naughty. And I got up and dressed and climbed out my window on to the shed without anybody knowing it. She'll never know the difference."

"Oh, Rosie," Maida said in a horrified tone, "Please never do it again." In spite of herself, Maida's eyes twinkled.

But Rosie only laughed. Maida watched her steal into her yard, watched her climb over the shed, watched her disappear through the window.

But she grieved over the matter as she walked home. Perhaps it was because she was thinking so deeply that she did not notice how quiet they all were in the living-room. But as she crossed the threshold, a pair of arms seized her and swung her into the air.

"Oh, papa, papa," she whispered, cuddling her face against his, "how glad I am to see you."

He marched with her over to the light.

"Well, little shop-keeper," he said after a long pause in which he studied her keenly, "you're beginning to look like a real live girl." He dropped her gently to her feet. "Now show me your shop."

CHAPTER V: PRIMROSE COURT

But during that first two weeks a continual rush of business made long days for Maida. All the children in the neighborhood were curious to see the place. It had been dark and dingy as long as they could remember. Now it was always bright and pretty--always sweet with the perfume of flowers, always gay with the music of birds. But more, the children wanted to see the lame little girl who "tended store," who seemed to try so hard to please her customers and who was so affectionate and respectful with the old, old lady whom she called "Granny."

At noon and night the bell sounded a continuous tinkle.

For a week Maida kept rather close to the shop. She wanted to get acquainted with all her customers. Moreover, she wanted to find out which of the things she had bought sold quickly and which were unpopular.

After a day or two her life fell into a regular programme.

Early in the morning she would put the shop to rights for the day's sale, dusting, replacing the things she had sold, rearranging them often according to some pretty new scheme.

About eight o'clock the bell would call her into the shop and it would be brisk work until nine. Then would come a rest of three hours, broken only by an occasional customer. In this interval she often worked in the yard, raking up the leaves that fell from vine and bush, picking the bravely-blooming dahlias, gathering sprays of woodbine for the vases, scattering crumbs to the birds.

At twelve the children would begin to flood the shop again and Maida would be on her feet constantly until two. Between two and four came another long rest. After school trade started up again. Often it lasted until six, when she locked the door for the night.

In her leisure moments she used to watch the people coming and going in Primrose Court. With Rosie's and Dicky's help, she soon knew everybody by name. She discovered by degrees that on the right side of the court lived the Hales, the Clarks, the Doyles and the Dores; on the left side, the Duncans, the Brines and the Allisons. In the big house at the back lived the Lathrops.

Betsy was a great delight to Maida, for the neighborhood brimmed with stories of her mischief. She had buried her best doll in the ash-barrel, thrown her mother's pocketbook down the cesspool, put all the clean laundry into a tub of water and painted the parlor fireplace with tomato catsup. In a single afternoon, having become secretly possessed of a pair of scissors, she cut all the fringe off the parlor furniture, cut great scallops in the parlor curtains, cut great patches of fur off the cat's back. When her mother found her, she was busy cutting her own hair.

Often Granny would hear the door slam on Maida's hurried rush from the shop. Hobbling to the window, she would see the child leading Betsy by the hand. "Running away again," was all Maida would say. Occasionally Maida would call in a vexed tone, "Now *how* did she creep past the window without my seeing her?" And outside would be rosy-cheeked, brass-buttoned Mr. Flanagan, carrying Betsy home. Once Billy arrived at the shop, bearing Betsy in his arms. "She was almost to the bridge," he said, "when I caught sight of her from the car window. The little tramp!"

Betsy never seemed to mind being caught. For an instant the little rosebud that was her mouth would part over the tiny pearls that were her teeth. This roguish smile seemed to say: "You wait until the next time. You won't catch me then."

Sometimes Betsy would come into the shop for an hour's play. Maida loved to have her there but it was like entertaining a whirlwind. Betsy had a strong curiosity to see what the drawers and boxes contained. Everything had to be put back in its place when she left.

Next to the Hales lived the Clarks. By the end of the first week Maida was the chief adoration of the Clark twins. Dorothy and Mabel were just as good as Betsy was naughty. When they came over to see Maida, they played quietly with whatever she chose to give them. It was an hour, ordinarily, before they could be made to talk above a whisper. If they saw Maida coming into the court, they would run to her side, slipping a hot little hand into each of hers. Attended always by this roly-poly bodyguard, Maida would limp from group to group of the playing children. Nobody in Primrose Court could tell the Clark twins apart. Maida soon learned the difference although she could never explain it to anybody else. "It's something you have to feel," she said.

Billy Potter enjoyed the twins as much as Maida did. "Good morning, Dorothy-Mabel," he always said when he met one of them; "is this you or your sister?" And he always answered their whispered remarks with whispers so much softer than theirs that he finally succeeded in forcing them to raise their shy little voices.

The Doyles and the Dores lived in one house next to the Clarks, Molly and Tim on the first floor, Dicky and Delia above. Maida became very fond of the Doyle children. Like Betsy, they were too young to go to school and she saw a good deal of them in the lonely school hours. The puddle was an endless source of amusement to them. As long as it remained, they entertained themselves playing along its shores.

"There's that choild in the water again," Granny would cry from the living-room.

Looking out, Maida would see Tim spread out on all fours. Like an obstinate little pig, he would lie still until Molly picked him up. She would take him home and in a few moments he would reappear in fresh, clean clothes again.

"Hello, Tim," Billy Potter would say whenever they met. "Fallen into a pud-muddle lately?"

The word ***pud-muddle*** always sent Tim off into peals of laughter. It was the only thing Maida had discovered that could make him laugh, for he was as serious as Molly was merry. Molly certainly was the jolliest little girl in the court--Maida had never seen her with anything but a smiling face.

Dicky's mother went to work so early and came back so late that Maida had never seen her. But Dicky soon became an intimate. Maida had begun the reading lessons and Dicky was so eager to get on that they were progressing famously.

The Lathrops lived in the big house at the back of the court. Granny learned from the Misses Allison that, formerly, the whole neighborhood had belonged to the Lathrop family. But they had sold all their land, piece by piece, except the one big lot on which the house stood. Perhaps it was because they had once been so important that Mrs. Lathrop seemed to feel herself a little better than the rest of the people in Primrose Court. At any rate, although she spoke with all, the Misses

Allison were the only ones on whom she condescended to call. Maida caught a glimpse of her occasionally on the piazza--a tall, thin woman, white-haired and sharp-featured, who always wore a worsted shawl.

The house was a big, bulky building, a mass of piazzas and bay-windows, with a hexagonal cupola on the top. It was painted white with green blinds and trimmed with a great deal of wooden lace. The wide lawn was well-kept and plots of flowers, here and there, gave it a gay air.

Laura had a brother named Harold, who was short and fat. Harold seemed to do nothing all day long but ride a wheel at a tearing pace over the asphalt paths, and regularly, for two hours every morning, to draw a shrieking bow across a tortured violin.

The more Maida watched Laura the less she liked her. She could see that what Rosie said was perfectly true--Laura put on airs. Every afternoon Laura played on the lawn. Her appearance was the signal for all the small fry of the neighborhood to gather about the gate. First would come the Doyles, then Betsy, then, one by one, the strange children who wandered into the court, until there would be a row of wistful little faces stuck between the bars of the fence. They would follow every move that Laura made as she played with the toys spread in profusion upon the grass.

Laura often pretended not to see them. She would lift her large family of dolls, one after another, from cradle to bed and from bed to tiny chair and sofa. She would parade up and down the walk, using first one doll-carriage, then the other. She would even play a game of croquet against herself. Occasionally she would call in a condescending tone, "You may come in for awhile if you wish, little children." And when the delighted little throng had scampered to her side, she would show them all her toy treasures on condition that they did not touch them.

When the proceedings reached this stage, Maida would be so angry that she could look no longer. Very often, after Laura had sent the children away, Maida would call them into the shop. She would let them play all the rest of the afternoon with anything her stock afforded.

On the right side of the court lived Arthur Duncan, the Misses Allison and Rosie Brine. The more Maida saw of Arthur, the more she disliked him. In fact, she hated to have him come into the shop. It seemed to her that he went out of his way to be impolite to her, that he looked at her with a decided expression of contempt in his big dark eyes. But Rosie and Dicky seemed very fond of him. Billy Potter had once told her that one good way of judging people was by the friends they made. If that were true, she had to acknowledge that there must be something fine about Arthur that she had not discovered.

Maida guessed that the W.M.N.T.'s met three or four times a week. Certainly there were very busy doings at Dicky's or at Arthur's house every other day. What it was all about, Maida did not know. But she fancied that it had much to do with Dicky's frequent purchases of colored tissue paper.

The Misses Allison had become great friends with Granny. Matilda, the blind sister, was very slender and sweet-faced. She sat all day in the window, crocheting the beautiful, fleecy shawls by which she helped support the household.

Jemima, the older, short, fat and with snapping black eyes, did the housework, attended to the parrot and waited by inches on her afflicted sister. Occasionally in the evening they would come to call on Granny. Billy Potter was very nice to them both. He was always telling the sisters the long amusing stories of his adventures. Miss Matilda's gentle face used positively to beam at these times, and Miss Jemima laughed so hard that, according to her own story, his talk put her "in stitches."

Maida did not see Rosie's mother often. To tell the truth, she was a little afraid of her. She was a tall, handsome, black-browed woman--a grown-up Rosie--with an appearance of great strength and of even greater temper. "Ah, that choild's the limb," Granny would say, when Maida brought her some new tale of Rosie's disobedience. And yet, in the curious way in which Maida divined things that were not told her, she knew that, next to Dicky, Rosie was Granny's favorite of all the children in the neighborhood.

With all these little people to act upon its stage, it is not surprising that Primrose Court seemed to Maida to be a little theater of fun--a stage to which her window was the royal box. Something was going on there from morning to night. Here would be a little group of little girls playing "house" with numerous families of dolls. There, it would be boys, gathered in an excited ring, playing marbles or top. Just before school, games like leap-frog, or tag or prisoners' base would prevail. But, later, when there was more time, hoist-the-sail would fill the air with its strange cries, or hide-and-seek would make the place boil with excitement. Maida used to watch these games wistfully, for Granny had decided that they were all too rough for her. She would not even let Maida play "London-Bridge-is-falling-down" or "drop the handkerchief"--anything, in fact, in which she would have to run or pull.

But Granny had no objections to the gentler fun of "Miss Jennie-I-Jones," "ring-a-ring-a-rounder," "water, water wildflower," "the farmer in the dell," "go in and out the windows." Maida used to try to pick out the airs of these games on the spinet--she never could decide which was the sweetest.

Maida soon learned how to play jackstones and, at the end of the second week, she was almost as proficient as Rosie with the top. The thing she most wanted to learn, however, was jump-rope. Every little girl in Primrose Court could jump-rope--even the twins, who were especially nimble at "pepper." Maida tried it one night--all alone in the shop. But suddenly her weak leg gave way under her and she fell to the floor. Granny, rushing in from the other room, scolded her violently. She ended by forbidding her to jump again without special permission. But Maida made up her mind that she was going to learn sometime, even, as she said with a roguish smile, "if it took a leg." She talked it over with Rosie.

"You let her jump just one jump every morning and night, Granny," Rosie advised, "and I'm sure it will be all right. That won't hurt her any and, after awhile, she'll find she can jump two, then three and so on. That's the way I learned."

Granny agreed to this. Maida practiced constantly, one jump in her nightgown, just before going to bed, and another, all dressed, just after she got up.

"I jumped three jumps this morning without failing, Granny," she said one morning at breakfast. Within a few days the record climbed to five, then to seven, then, at a leap, to ten.

Dr. Pierce called early one morning. His eyes opened wide when they fell upon her. "Well, well, Pinkwink," he said. "What do you mean by bringing me way over here! I thought you were supposed to be a sick young person. Where'd you get that color?"

A flush like that of a pink sweet-pea blossom had begun to show in Maida's cheek. It was faint but it was permanent.

"Why, you're the worst fraud on my list. If you keep on like this, young woman, I shan't have any excuse for calling. You've done fine, Granny."

Granny looked, as Dr. Pierce afterwards said, "as tickled as Punch."

"How do you like shop-keeping?" Dr. Pierce went on.

"Like it!" Maida plunged into praise so swift and enthusiastic that Dr. Pierce told her to go more slowly or he would put a bit in her mouth. But he listened attentively. "Well, I see you're not tired of it," he commented.

"Tired!" Maida's indignation was so intense that Dr. Pierce shook until every curl bobbed.

"And I get so hungry," she went on. "You see I have to wait until two o'clock sometimes before I can get my lunch, because from twelve to two are my busy hours. Those days it seems as if the school bell would never ring."

"Sure, tis a foine little pig OI'm growing now," Granny said.

"And as for sleeping--" Maida stopped as if there were no words anywhere to describe her condition.

Granny finished it for her. "The choild sleeps like a top."

Billy Potter came at least every day and sometimes oftener. Every child in Primrose Court knew him by the end of the first week and every child loved him by the end of the second. And they all called him Billy. He would not let them call him Mr. Potter or even Uncle Billy because, he said, he was a child when he was with them and he wanted to be treated like a child. He played all their games with a skill that they thought no mere grown-up could possess. Like Rosie, he seemed to be bubbling over with life and spirits. He was always running, leaping, jumping, climbing, turning cartwheels and somersaults, vaulting fences and "chinning" himself unexpectedly whenever he came to a doorway.

"Oh, Masther Billy, 'tis the choild that you are!" Granny would say, twinkling.

"Yes, ma'am," Billy would answer.

At the end of the first fortnight, the neighborhood had accepted Granny and Maida as the mother-in-law and daughter of a "traveling man." From the beginning Granny had seemed one of them, but Maida was a puzzle. The children could not understand how a little girl could be grown-up and babyish at the same time. And if you stop to think it over, perhaps you can understand how they felt.

Here was a child who had never played, "London-Bridge-is-falling-down" or jackstones or jump-rope or hop-scotch. Yet she talked familiarly of automobiles, yachts and horses. She knew nothing about geography and yet, her conversation was full of such phrases as "The spring we were in Paris" or "The winter we spent in Rome." She knew nothing about nouns and verbs but she talked Italian fluently with the hand-organ man who came every week and many of her books were in French. She knew nothing about fractions or decimals, yet she referred familiarly to "drawing checks," to gold eagles and to Wall Street. Her writing was so bad that the children made fun of it, yet she could spin off a letter of eight pages in a flash. And she told the most wonderful fairy-tales that had ever been heard in Primrose Court.

Because of all these things the children had a kind of contempt for her mingled with a curious awe.

She was so polite with grown people that it was fairly embarrassing. She always arose from her chair when they entered the room, always picked up the things they dropped and never interrupted. And yet she could carry on a long conversation with them. She never said, "Yes, ma'am," or "No, ma'am." Instead, she said, "Yes, Mrs. Brine," or "No, Miss Allison," and she looked whomever she was talking with straight in the eye.

She would play with the little children as willingly as with the bigger ones. Often when the older girls and boys were in school, she would bring out a lapful of toys and spend the whole morning with the little ones. When Granny called her, she would give all the toys away, dividing them with a careful justice. And, yet, whenever children bought things of her in the shop, she always expected them to pay the whole price. You can see how the neighborhood would fairly buzz with talk about her.

As for Maida--with all this newness of friend-making and out-of-doors games, it is not to be wondered that her head was a jumble at the end of each day. In that delicious, dozy interval before she fell asleep at night, all kinds of pretty pictures seemed to paint themselves on her eyelids.

Now it was Rose-Red swaying like a great overgrown scarlet flower from the bars of a lamp-post. Now it was Dicky hoisting himself along on his crutches, his face alight with his radiant smile. Now it was a line of laughing, rosy-cheeked children, as long as the tail of a kite, pelting to goal at the magic cry "Liberty poles are bending!" Or it was a group of little girls, setting out rows and rows of bright-colored paper-dolls among the shadows of one of the deep old doorways. But always in a few moments came the sweetest kind of sleep. And always through her dreams flowed the plaintive music of "Go in and out the windows." Often she seemed to wake in the morning to the Clarion cry, "Hoist the sail!"

It did not seem to Maida that the days were long enough to do all the things she wanted to do.

CHAPTER VI: TWO CALLS

One morning, Laura Lathrop came bustling importantly into the shop. "Good morning, Maida," she said; "you may come over to my house this afternoon and play with me if you'd like."

"Thank you, Laura," Maida answered. To anybody else, she would have added, "I shall be delighted to come." But to Laura, she only said, "It is kind of you to ask me."

"From about two until four," Laura went on in her most superior tone. "I suppose you can't get off for much longer than that."

"Granny is always willing to wait on customers if I want to play," Maida explained, "but I think she would not want me to stay longer than that, anyway."

"Very well, then. Shall we say at two?" Laura said this with a very grown-up air. Maida knew that she was imitating her mother.

Laura had scarcely left when Dicky appeared, swinging between his crutches. "Maida," he said, "I want you to come over to-morrow afternoon and see my place. You've not seen Delia yet and there's a whole lot of things I want to show you. I'm going to clean house to-day so's I'll be all ready for you to-morrow."

"Oh, thank you," Maida said. The sparkle that always meant delight came into her face. "I shall be delighted. I've always wanted to go over and see you ever since I first knew you. But Granny said to wait until you invited me. And I really have never seen Delia except when Rosie's had her in the carriage. And then she's always been asleep."

"You have to see Delia in the house to know what a naughty baby she is," Dicky said. He spoke as if that were the finest tribute that he could pay his little sister.

"Granny," Maida said that noon at lunch, "Laura Lathrop came here and invited me to come to see her this afternoon and I just hate the thought of going--I don't know why. Then Dicky came and invited me to come and see him to-morrow afternoon and I just love the thought of going. Isn't it strange?"

"Very," Granny said, smiling. "But you be sure to be a noice choild this afternoon, no matter what that wan says to you."

Granny always referred to Laura as "that wan."

"Oh, yes, I'll be good, Granny. Isn't it funny," Maida went on. The tone of her voice showed that she was thinking hard. "Laura makes me mad--oh, just hopping mad,"--"hopping mad" was one of Rosie's expressions--"and yet it seems to me I'd die before I'd let her know it."

Laura was waiting for her on the piazza when Maida presented herself at the Lathrop door. "Won't you come in and take your things off, first?" she said. "I thought we'd play in the house for awhile."

She took Maida immediately upstairs to her bedroom--a large room all furnished in blue--blue paper, blue bureau scarf covered with lace, blue bed-spread covered with lace, a big, round, blue roller where the pillows should be.

"How do you like my room, Maida?"

"It's very pretty."

"This is my toilet-set." Laura pointed to the glittering articles on the bureau. "Papa's given them to me, one piece at a time. It's all of silver and every thing has my initials on it. What is your set of?"

Laura paused before she asked this last question and darted one of her sideways looks at Maida. "She thinks I haven't any toilet-set and she wants to make me say so," Maida thought. "Ivory," she said aloud.

"Ivory! I shouldn't think that would be very pretty."

Laura opened her bureau drawers, one at a time, and showed Maida the pretty clothes packed in neat piles there. She opened the large closet and displayed elaborately-made frocks, suspended on hangers. And all the time, with little sharp, sideways glances, she was studying the effect on Maida. But Maida's face betrayed none of the wonder and envy that Laura evidently expected. Maida was very polite but it was evident that she was not much interested.

Next they went upstairs to a big playroom which covered the whole top of the house. Shelves covered with books and toys lined the walls. A fire, burning in the big fireplace, made it very cheerful.

"Oh, what a darling doll-house," Maida exclaimed, pausing before the miniature mansion, very elegantly furnished.

"Oh, do you like it?" Laura beamed with pride.

"I just love it! Particularly because it's so little."

"Little!" Laura bristled. "I don't think it's so very little. It's the biggest doll-house I ever saw. Did you ever see a bigger one?"

Maida looked embarrassed. "Only one."

"Whose was it?"

"It was the one my father had built for me at Pride's. It was too big to be a doll's house. It was really a small cottage. There were four rooms--two upstairs and two downstairs and a staircase that you could really walk up. But I don't like it half so well as this one," Maida went on truthfully. "I think it's very queer but, somehow, the smaller things are the better I like them. I guess it's because I've seen so many big things."

Laura looked impressed and puzzled at the same time. "And you really could walk up the stairs? Let's go up in the cupola," she suggested, after an uncertain interval in which she seemed to think of nothing else to show.

The stairs at the end of the playroom led into the cupola. Maida exclaimed with delight over the view which she saw from the windows. On one side was the river with the draw-bridge, the Navy Yard and the monument on Bunker Hill. On the other stretched the smoky expanse of Boston with the golden dome of the state house gleaming in the midst of a huge, red-brick huddle.

"Did you have a cupola at Pride's Crossing?" Laura asked triumphantly.

"Oh, no--how I wish I had!"

Laura beamed again.

"Laura likes to have things other people haven't," Maida thought.

Her hostess now conducted her back over the two flights of stairs to the lower floor. They went into the dining-room, which was all shining oak and glittering cut-glass; into the parlor, which was filled with gold furniture, puffily upholstered in blue brocade; into the libraries, which Maida liked best of all, because there were so many books and--

"Oh, oh, oh!" she exclaimed, stopping before one of the pictures; "that's Santa Maria in Cosmedin. I haven't seen that since I left Rome."

"How long did you stay in Rome, little girl?" a voice asked back of her. Maida turned. Mrs. Lathrop had come into the room.

Maida arose immediately from her chair. "We stayed in Rome two months," she said.

"Indeed. And where else did you go?"

"London, Paris, Florence and Venice."

"Do you know these other pictures?" Mrs. Lathrop asked. "I've been collecting photographs of Italian churches."

Maida went about identifying the places with little cries of joy. "Ara Coeli--I saw in there the little wooden bambino who cures sick people. It's so covered with bracelets and rings and lockets and pins and chains that grateful people have given it that it looks as if it were dressed in jewels. The bambino's such a darling little thing with such a sweet look in its face. That's St. Agnes outside the wall--I saw two dear little baby lambs blessed on the altar there on St. Agnes's day. One was all covered with red garlands and the other with green. Oh, they were such sweethearts! They were going to use the fleece to make some garment for the pope. That's Santa Maria della Salute--they call it Santa Maria della **Volute** instead of **Salute** because it's all covered with volutes." Maida smiled sunnily into Mrs. Lathrop's face as if expecting sympathy with this architectural joke.

But Mrs. Lathrop did not smile. She looked a little staggered. She studied Maida for a long time out of her shrewd, light eyes.

"Whose family did you travel with?" she asked at last.

Maida felt a little embarrassed. If Mrs. Lathrop asked her certain questions, it would place her in a very uncomfortable position. On the one hand, Maida could not tell a lie. On the other, her father had told her to tell nobody that she was his daughter.

"The family of Mr. Jerome Westabrook," she said at last.

"Oh!" It was the "oh" of a person who is much impressed. "'Buffalo' Westabrook?" Mrs. Lathrop asked.

"Yes."

"Did your grandmother, Mrs. Flynn, go with you?"

"Yes."

Mrs. Lathrop continued to look very hard at Maida. Her eyes wandered over the little blue frock--simple but of the best materials--over the white "tire" of a delicate plaided nainsook, trimmed with Valenciennes lace, the string of blue Venetian beads, the soft, carefully-fitted shoes.

"Mr. Westabrook has a little girl, hasn't he?" Mrs. Lathrop said.

Maida felt extremely uncomfortable now. But she looked Mrs. Lathrop straight in the eye. "Yes," she answered.

"About your age?"

"Yes."

"She is an invalid, isn't she?"

"She *was*," Maida said with emphasis.

Mrs. Lathrop did not ask any more questions. She went presently into the back library. An old gentleman sat there, reading.

"That little girl who keeps the store at the corner is in there, playing with Laura, father," she said. "I guess her grandmother was a servant in 'Buffalo' Westabrook's family, for they traveled abroad a year with the Westabrook family. Evidently, they give her all the little Westabrook girl's clothes--she's dressed quite out of keeping with her station in life. Curious how refinement rubs off--the child has really a good deal of manner. I don't know that I quite like to have Laura playing with her, though."

The two little girls returned after awhile to the playroom.

"How would you like to have me dance for you?" Laura asked abruptly. "You know I take fancy dancing."

"Oh, Laura," Maida said delightedly "will you?"

"Of course I will," Laura said with her most beaming expression. "You wait here while I go downstairs and get into my costume. Watch that door, for I shall make my entrance there."

Maida waited what seemed a long time to her. Then suddenly Laura came whirling into the room. She had put on a little frock of pale-blue liberty silk that lay, skirt, bodice and tiny sleeves, in many little pleats--"accordion-pleated," Laura afterwards described it. Laura's neck and arms were bare. She wore blue silk stockings and little blue-kid slippers, heelless and tied across the ankles with ribbons. Her hair hung in a crimpy torrent to below her waist.

"Oh, Laura, how lovely you do look!" Maida said, "I think you're perfectly beautiful!"

Laura smiled. Lifting both arms above her head, she floated about the room, dancing on the very tips of her toes. Turning and smiling over her shoulder, she bent and swayed and attitudinized. Maida could have watched her forever.

In a few moments she disappeared again. This time she came back in a red-silk frock with a little bolero jacket of black velvet, hung with many tinkling coins. Whenever her fingers moved, a little pretty clapping sound came from them--Maida discovered that she carried tiny wooden clappers. Whenever her heels came together, a pretty musical clink came from them--Maida discovered that on her shoes were tiny metal plates.

Once again Laura went out. This time, she returned dressed like a little sailor boy. She danced a gay little hornpipe.

"I never saw anything so marvelous in my life," Maida said, her eyes shining with enjoyment. "Oh, Laura how I wish I could dance like that. How did you ever learn? Do you practice all the time?"

"Oh, it's not so very hard--for me," Laura returned. "Of course, everybody couldn't learn. And I suppose you, being lame, could never do anything at all."

This was the first allusion that had been made in Primrose Court to Maida's lameness. Her face shadowed a little. "No, I'm afraid I couldn't," she said regretfully. "But--oh--think what a lovely dancer Rosie would make."

"I'm afraid Rosie's too rough," Laura said. She unfolded a little fan and began fanning herself languidly. "It's a great bother sometimes," she went on in a bored tone of voice. "Everybody is always asking me to dance at their parties. I danced at a beautiful May party last year. Did you ever see a May-pole?"

"Oh, yes," Maida said. "My birthday comes on May Day and last year father gave me a party. He had a May-pole set up on the lawn and all the children danced about it."

"My birthday comes in the summer, too. I always have a party on our place in Marblehead," Laura said. "I had fifty children at my party last year. How many did you have?"

"We sent out over five hundred invitations, I believe. But not quite four hundred accepted."

"Four hundred," Laura repeated. "Goodness, what could so many children do?"

"Oh, there were all sorts of things for them to do," Maida answered. "There was archery and diabolo and croquet and fishing-ponds and a merry-go-round and Punch and Judy on the lawn and a play in my little theater--I can't remember everything."

Laura's eyes had grown very big. "Didn't you have a perfectly splendiferous time?" she asked.

"No, not particularly," Maida said. "Not half such a good time as I've had playing in Primrose Court. I wasn't very well and then, somehow, I didn't care for those children the way I care for Dicky and Rosie and the court children."

"Goodness!" was all Laura could say for a moment. But finally she added, "I don't believe that, Maida!"

Maida stared at her and started to speak. "Oh, there's the clock striking four?" was all she said though. "I must go. Thank you for dancing for me."

She flew into her coat and hat. She could not seem to get away quick enough. Nobody had ever doubted her word before. She could not exactly explain it to herself but she felt if she talked with Laura another moment, she would fly out of her skin.

"Mother," Laura said, after Maida had gone, "Maida Flynn told me that her father gave her a birthday party last year and invited five hundred children to it and they had a theater and a Punch and Judy show and all sorts of things. Do you think it's true?"

Mrs. Lathrop set her lips firmly. "No, I think it is probably not true. I think you'd better not play with the little Flynn girl any more."

The next afternoon, Maida went, as she had promised, to see Dicky.

She could see at a glance that Mrs. Dore was having a hard struggle to support her little family. In the size and comfort of its furnishings, the place was the exact opposite of the Lathrop home. But, somehow, there was a wonderful feeling of home there.

"Dicky, how do you manage to keep so clean here?" Maida asked in genuine wonder.

And indeed, hard work showed everywhere. The oilcloth shone like glass. The stove was as clean as a newly-polished shoe. The rows of pans on the wall fairly twinkled. Delicious smells were filling the air. Maida guessed that Dicky was making one of the Irish stews that were his specialty.

"See that little truck over there?" Dicky said. "That helps a lot. Arthur Duncan made that for me. You see we have to keep our coal in that closet, way across the room. I used to get awful tired filling the coal-hod and lugging it over to the stove. But now you see I fill that truck at the closet, wheel it over to the stove and I don't have to think of coal for three days."

"Arthur must be a very clever boy," Maida said thoughtfully.

"You bet he is. See that tin can in the sink? Well, I wanted a soap-shaker but couldn't afford to get one. Arthur took that can and punched the bottom full of holes. I keep it filled up with all the odds and ends of soap. When I wash the dishes, I just let the boiling water from the kettle flow through it. It makes water grand and soapy. Arthur made me that iron dish-rag and that dish-mop."

A sleepy cry came from the corner. Dicky swung across the room. Balancing himself against the cradle there, he lifted the baby to the floor. "She can't walk yet but you watch her go," he said proudly.

Go! The baby crept across the room so fast that Maida had to run to keep up with her. "Oh, the love!" she said, taking Delia into her arms. "Think of having a whole baby to yourself."

"Can't leave a thing round where she is," Dicky said proudly, as if this were the best thing he could say about her. "Have to put *my* work away the moment she wakes up. Isn't she a buster, though?"

"I should say she was!" And indeed, the baby was as fat as a little partridge. Maida wondered how Dicky could lift her. Also Delia was as healthy-looking as Dicky was sickly. Her cheeks showed a pink that was almost purple and her head looked like a mop, so thickly was it overgrown with tangled, red-gold curls.

"Is she named after your mother?" Maida asked.

"No--after my grandmother in Ireland. But of course we don't call her anything but 'baby' yet. My, but she's a case! If I didn't watch her all the time, every pan in this room would be on the floor in a jiffy. And she tears everything she puts her hands on."

"Granny must see her sometime--Granny's name is Delia."

"Hi, stop that!" Dicky called. For Delia had discovered the little bundle that Maida had placed on a chair, and was busy trying to tear it open.

"Let her open it," Maida said, "I brought it for her."

They watched.

It took a long time, but Delia sat down, giving her whole attention to it. Finally her busy fingers pulled off so much paper that a pair of tiny rubber dolls dropped into her lap.

"Say 'Thank you, Maida,'" Dicky prompted.

Delia said something and Dicky assured her that the baby had obeyed him. It sounded like, "Sank-oo-Maysa."

While Delia occupied herself with the dolls, Maida listened to Dicky's reading lesson. He was getting on beautifully now. At least he could puzzle out by himself some of the stories that Maida lent him. When they had finished that day's fairy-tale, Dicky said:

"Did you ever see a peacock, Maida?"

"Oh, yes--a great many."

"Where?"

"I saw ever so many in the Jardin des Plantes in Paris and then my father has some in his camp in the Adirondacks."

"Has he many?"

"A dozen."

"I'm just wild to see one. Are they as beautiful as that picture in the fairy-tale?"

"They're as beautiful as--as--" Maida groped about in her mind to find something to compare them to "--as angels," she said at last.

"And do they really open their tails like a fan?"

"That is the most wonderful sight, Dicky, that you ever saw." Maida's manner was almost solemn. "When they unfurl the whole fan and the sun shines on all the green and blue eyes and on all the little gold feathers, it's so beautiful. Well, it makes you ache. I *cried* the first time I saw one. And when their fans are down, they carry them so daintily, straight out, not a single feather trailing on the ground. There are two white peacocks on the Adirondacks place."

" *White* peacocks! I never heard of white ones."

"They're not common."

"Think of seeing a dozen peacocks every day!" Dicky exclaimed. "Jiminy crickets! Why, Maida, your life must have been just like a fairy-tale when you lived there."

"It seems more like a fairy-tale here."

They laughed at this difference of opinion.

"Dicky," Maida asked suddenly, "do you know that Rosie steals out of her window at night sometimes when her mother doesn't know it?"

"Sure--I know that. You see," he went on to explain, "it's like this. Rosie is an awful bad girl in some ways--there's no doubt about that. But my mother says Rosie isn't as bad as she seems. My mother says Rosie's mother has never learned how to manage her. She whips Rosie an awful lot. And the more she whips Rosie, the naughtier she gets. Rosie says she's going to run away some day, and by George, I bet she'll do it. She always does what she says she'll do."

"Isn't it dreadful?" Maida said in a frightened tone. "Run away! I never heard of such a thing. Think of having a mother and then not getting along with her. Suppose she died sometime, as my mother did."

"I don't know what I'd do without my mother," Dicky said thoughtfully. "But then I've got the best mother that ever was. I wish she didn't have to work so hard. But you wait until I get on my feet. Then you'll see how I'm going to earn money for her."

When Maida got home that night, Billy Potter sat with Granny in the living-room. Maida came in so quietly that they took no notice of her. Granny was talking. Maida could see that the tears were coursing down the wrinkles in her cheeks.

"And after that, the poor choild ran away to America and I niver have seen her since. Her father died repenting av his anger aginst her. But ut was too late. At last, in me old age, Oi came over to America, hoping Oi cud foind her. But, glory be, Oi had no idea 'twas such a big place! And Oi've hunted and Oi've hunted and Oi've hunted. But niver a track of her cud Oi foind--me little Annie!"

Billy's face was all screwed up, but it was not with laughter. "Did you ever speak to Mr. Westabrook about it?"

"Oh, Misther Westabruk done iv'ry t'ing he cud--the foine man that he is. Ad-ver *tise* ments and *de* tayktives, but wid all his money, he cudn't foind out a t'ing. If ut wasn't for my blissed lamb, I'd pray to the saints to let me die."

Maida knew what they were talking about--Granny had often told her the sad story of her lost daughter.

"What town in Ireland did you live in, Granny?" Billy asked.

"Aldigarey, County Sligo." "Now don't you get discouraged, Granny," Billy said, "I'm going to find your daughter for you."

He jumped to his feet and walked about the room. "I'm something of a detec-tive myself, and you'll see I'll make good on this job if it takes twenty years."

"Oh, Billy, do--please do," Maida burst in. "It will make Granny so happy."

Granny seemed happier already. She dried her tears.

"'Tis the good b'y ye are, Misther Billy," she said gratefully.

"Yes, m'm," said Billy.

CHAPTER VII: TROUBLE

The next week was a week of trouble for Maida. Everything seemed to go wrong from the first tinkle of the bell, Monday morning, to the last tinkle Saturday night.

It began with a conversation.

Rosie came marching in early Monday, head up, eyes flaming.

"Maida," she began at once, in her quickest, briskest tone, "I've got something to tell you. Laura Lathrop came over to Dicky's house the other day while the W.M.N.T.'s were meeting and she told us the greatest mess of stuff about you. I told her I was coming right over and tell you about it and she said, 'All right, you can.' Laura said that you said that last summer you had a birthday party that you invited five hundred children to. She said that you said that you had a May-pole at this party and a fish pond and a Punch and Judy show and all sorts of things. She said that you said that you had a big doll-house and a little theater all your own. I said that I didn't believe that you told her all that. Did you?"

"Oh, yes, I told her that--and more," Maida answered directly.

"Laura said it was all a pack of lies, but I don't believe that. Is it all true?"

"It's all true," Maida said.

Rosie looked at her hard. "You know, Maida," she went on after awhile, "you told me about a lot of birds and animals that your father had. I thought he kept a bird-place. But Dicky says you told him that your father had twelve peacocks, not in a store, but in a place where he lives." She paused and looked inquiringly at Maida.

Maida answered the look. "Yes, I told him that."

"And it's all true?" Rosie asked again.

"Yes, it's all true," Maida repeated.

Rosie hesitated a moment. "Harold Lathrop says that you're daffy."

Maida said nothing.

"Arthur Duncan says," Rosie went on more timidly, "that you probably dreamed those things."

Still Maida said nothing.

"Do you think you did dream them, Maida?"

Maida smiled. "No, I didn't dream them."

"Well, I thought of another thing," Rosie went on eagerly. "Miss Allison told mother that Granny told her that you'd been sick for a long time. And I thought, maybe you were out of your head and imagined those things. Oh, Maida," Rosie's voice actually coaxed her to favor this theory, "don't you think you imagined them?"

Maida laughed. "No, Rosie," she said in her quietest voice, "I did not imagine them."

For a moment neither of the two little girls spoke. But they stared, a little defiantly, into each other's eyes.

"What did Dicky say?" Maida asked after awhile.

"Oh, Dicky said he would believe anything you told him, no matter what it was. Dicky says he believes you're a princess in disguise--like in fairy-tales."

"Dear, dear Dicky!" Maida said. "He was the first friend I made in Primrose Court and I guess he's the best one."

"Well, I guess I'm your friend," Rosie said, firing up; "I told that little smarty-cat of a Laura if she ever said one word against you, I'd slap her good and hard. Only--only--it seems strange that a little girl who's just like the rest of us should have story-book things happening to her all the time. If it's true--then fairy-tales are true." She paused and looked Maida straight in the eye. "I can't believe it, Maida. But I know you believe it. And that's all there is to it. But you'd better believe I'm your friend."

Saying which she marched out.

Maida's second trouble began that night.

It had grown dark. Suddenly, without any warning, the door of the shop flew open. For an instant three or four voices filled the place with their yells. Then the door shut. Nothing was heard but the sound of running feet.

Granny and Maida rushed to the door. Nobody was in sight.

"Who was it? What does it mean, Granny?" Maida asked in bewilderment. "Only naughty b'ys, taysing you," Granny explained.

Maida had hardly seated herself when the performance was repeated. Again she rushed to the door. Again she saw nobody. The third time she did not stir from her chair.

Tuesday night the same thing happened. Who the boys were Maida could not find out. Why they bothered her, she could not guess.

"Take no notuce av ut, my lamb," Granny counselled. "When they foind you pay no attintion to ut, they'll be afther stopping."

Maida followed Granny's advice. But the annoyance did not cease and she began to dread the twilight. She made up her mind that she must put an end to it soon. She knew she could stop it at once by appealing to Billy Potter. And, yet, somehow, she did not want to ask for outside help. She had a feeling of pride about handling her own troubles.

One afternoon Laura came into the shop. It was the first time that Maida had seen her since the afternoon of her call and Maida did not speak. She felt that she could not have anything to do with Laura after what had happened. But she looked straight at Laura and waited.

Laura did not speak either. She looked at Maida as if she had never seen her before. She carried her head at its highest and she moved across the room with her most important air. As she stood a moment gazing at the things in the show case, she had never seemed more patronizing.

"A cent's worth of dulse, please," she said airily.

"Dulse?" Maida repeated questioningly; "I guess I haven't any. What is dulse?"

"Haven't any dulse?" Laura repeated with an appearance of being greatly shocked. "Do you mean to say you haven't any dulse?"

Maida did not answer--she put her lips tight together.

"This is a healthy shop," Laura went on in a sneering tone, "no mollolligobs, no apple-on-the-stick, no tamarinds, no pop-corn balls, no dulse. Why don't you sell the things we want? Half the children in the neighborhood are going down to Main Street to get them now."

She bustled out of the shop. Maida stared after her with wide, alarmed eyes.

For a moment she did not stir. Then she ran into the living-room and buried her face in Granny's lap, bursting into tears.

"Oh, Granny," she sobbed, "Laura Lathrop says that half the children don't like my shop and they're going down to Main Street to buy things. What shall I do? What shall I do?"

"There, there, acushla," Granny said soothingly, taking the trembling little girl on to her lap. "Don't worry about anny t'ing that wan says. 'Tis a foine little shop you have, as all the grown folks says."

"But, Granny," Maida protested passionately, "I don't want to please the grown people, I want to please the children. And papa said I must make the store pay. And now I'm afraid I never will. Oh, what shall I do?"

She got no further. A tinkle of the bell, followed by pattering footsteps, interrupted. In an instant, Rosie, brilliant in her scarlet cape and scarlet hat, with cheeks and lips the color of cherries, stood at her side.

"I saw that hateful Laura come out of here," she said. "I just knew she'd come in to make trouble. What did she say to you?"

Maida told her slowly between her sobs.

"Horrid little smarty-cat!" was Rosie's comment and she scowled until her face looked like a thunder-cloud.

"I shall never speak to her again," Maida declared fervently. "But what shall I do about it, Rosie?--it may be true what she said."

"Now don't you get discouraged, Maida," Rosie said. "Because I can tell you just how to get or make those things Laura spoke of."

"Oh, can you, Rosie. What would I do without you? I'll put everything down in a book so that I shan't forget them."

She limped over to the desk. There the black head bent over the golden one.

"What is dulse?" Maida demanded first.

"Don't you know what dulse is?" Rosie asked incredulously. "Maida, you are the queerest child. The commonest things you don't know anything about. And yet I suppose if I asked you if you'd seen a flying-machine, you'd say you had."

"I have," Maida answered instantly, "in Paris."

Rosie's face wrinkled into its most perplexed look. She changed the subject at once. "Well, dulse is a purple stuff--when you see a lot of it together, it looks as if a million toy-balloons had burst. It's all wrinkled up and tastes salty."

Maida thought hard for a moment. Then she burst into laughter, although the big round tear-drops were still hanging from the tips of her lashes. "There was a whole drawerful here when I first came. I remember now I thought it was waste stuff and threw it all away."

Rosie laughed too. "The tamarinds you can get from the man who comes round with the wagon. Mrs. Murdock used to make her own apples-on-the-stick, mollolligobs and corn-balls. I've helped her many a time. Now I'll write you a list of stuff to order from the grocer. I'll come round after school and we'll make a batch of all those things. To-night you get Billy to print a sign, '*apples on the stick and mollolligobs to-day*.' You put that in the window to-morrow morning and by to-morrow night, you'll be all sold out."

"Oh, Rosie," Maida said happily, "I shall be so much obliged to you!"

Rosie was as good as her word. She appeared that afternoon wearing a long-sleeved apron under the scarlet cape. It seemed to Maida that she worked like lightning, for she made batch after batch of candy, moving as capably about the stove as an experienced cook. In the meantime, Maida was popping corn at the fireplace. They mounted fifty apples on skewers and dipped them, one at a time, into the boiling candy. They made thirty corn-balls and twenty-five mollolligobs, which turned out to be round chunks of candy, stuck on the end of sticks.

"I never did see such clever children anywhere as there are in Primrose Court," Maida said that night with a sigh to Granny. "Rosie told me that she could make six kinds of candy. And Dicky can cook as well as his mother. They make me feel so useless. Why, Granny, I can't do a single thing that's any good to anybody."

The next day the shop was crowded. By night there was not an apple, a corn-ball or a mollolligob left.

"I shall have a sale like this once a week in the future," Maida said. "Why, Granny, lots and lots of children came here who'd never been in the shop before."

And so what looked like serious trouble ended very happily.

Trouble number three was a great deal more serious and it did not, at first, promise to end well at all. It had to do with Arthur Duncan. It had been going on for a week before Maida mentioned it to anybody. But it haunted her very dreams.

Early Monday morning, Arthur came into the shop. In his usual gruff voice and with his usual surly manner, he said, "Show me some of those rubbers in the window."

Maida took out a handful of the rubbers--five, she thought--and put them on the counter. While Arthur looked them over, she turned to replace a paper-doll which she had knocked down.

"Guess I won't take one to-day," Arthur said, while her back was still turned, and walked out.

When Maida put the rubbers back, she discovered that there were only four. She made up her mind that she had not counted right and thought no more of the incident.

Two days later, Arthur Duncan came in again. Maida had just been selling some pencils--pretty striped ones with a blue stone in the end. Three of them were left lying out on the counter. Arthur asked her to show him some penholders. Maida took three from the shelves back of her. He bought one of these. After he had gone, she discovered that there were only two pencils left on the counter.

"One of them must have rolled off," Maida thought. But although she looked everywhere, she could not find it. The incident of the rubber occurred to her. She felt a little troubled but she resolved to put both circumstances out of her mind.

A day or two later, Arthur Duncan came in for the third time. It happened that Granny was out marketing.

Piled on the counter was a stack of blank-books--pretty books they were, with a child's head in color on the cover. Arthur asked for letter-paper. Maida turned back to the shelf. With her hand on the sliding door, she stopped, half-stunned.

Reflected in the glass she saw Arthur Duncan stow one of the blank books away in his pocket.

Maida felt sick all over. She did not know what to do. She did not know what to say.

She fumbled with trembling hands among the things on the shelf. She dreaded to turn for fear her face would express what she had seen.

"Perhaps he'll pay for it," she thought; "I hope he will."

But Arthur made no offer to pay. He looked over the letter-paper that Maida, with downcast eyes, put before him, decided that he did not want any after all, and walked coolly from the shop.

Granny, coming in a few moments later, was surprised to find Maida leaning on the counter, her face buried in her hands.

"What's the matter with my lamb?" the old lady asked cheerfully.

"Nothing, Granny," Maida said. But she did not meet Granny's eye and during dinner she was quiet and serious.

That night Billy Potter called. "Well, how goes the **Bon Marche of** Charlestown?" he asked cheerfully.

"Billy," Maida said gravely, "if you found that a little boy--I can't say what his name is--was stealing from you, what would you do?"

Billy considered the question as gravely as she had asked it. "Tell the policeman on the beat and get him to throw a scare into him," he said at last.

"I guess that's what I'll have to do." But Maida's tone was mournful.

But Granny interrupted.

"Don't you do ut, my lamb--don't you do ut!" She turned to them both--they had never seen her blue eyes so fiery before. "Suppose you was one av these poor little chilthren that lives round here that's always had harrd wurruds for their meals and hunger for their pillow, wudn't you be afther staling yersilf if ut came aisy-loike and nobody was luking?"

Neither Billy nor Maida spoke for a moment.

"I guess Granny's right," Billy said finally.

"I guess she is," Maida said with a sigh.

It was three days before Arthur Duncan came into the shop again. But in the meantime, Maida went one afternoon to play with Dicky. Dicky was drawing at a table when Maida came in. She glanced at his work. He was using a striped pencil with a blue stone in its end, a blank-book with the picture of a little girl on the cover, a rubber of a kind very familiar to her. Maida knew certainly that Dicky had bought none of these things from her. She knew as certainly that they were the things Arthur Duncan had stolen. What was the explanation of the mystery? She went to bed that night miserably unhappy.

Her heart beat pit-a-pat the next time she saw Arthur open the door. She folded her hands close together so that he should not see that she was trembling. She began to wish that she had followed Billy's advice. Sitting in the shop all alone--Granny, it happened again, was out--it occurred to her that it was, perhaps, too serious a situation for a little girl to deal with.

She had made up her mind that when Arthur was in the shop, she would not turn her back to him. She was determined not to give him the chance to fall into temptation. But he asked for pencil-sharpeners and pencil-sharpeners were kept in the lower drawer. There was nothing for her to do but to get down on the floor. She remembered with a sense of relief that she had left no stock out on the counter. She knelt upright on the floor, seeking for the box. Suddenly, reflected in the glass door, she saw another terrifying picture.

Arthur Duncan's arm was just closing the money drawer.

For an instant Maida felt so sick at heart that she wanted to run back into the living-room, throw herself into Granny's big chair and cry her eyes out. Then suddenly all this weakness went. A feeling, such as she had never known, came into its place. She was still angry but she was singularly cool. She felt no more afraid of Arthur Duncan than of the bowl of dahlias, blooming on the counter.

She whirled around in a flash and looked him straight in the eye.

"If there is anything in this shop that you want so much that you are willing to steal, tell me what it is and I'll give it to you," she said.

"Aw, what are you talking about?" Arthur demanded. He attempted to out-stare her.

But Maida kept her eyes steadily on his. "You know what I'm talking about well enough," she said quietly. "In the last week you've stolen a rubber and a pencil and a blank-book from me and just now you tried to take some money from the money-drawer."

Arthur sneered. "How are you going to prove it?" he asked impudently.

Maida was thoroughly angry. But something inside warned her that she must not give way to temper. For all her life, she had been accustomed to think before she spoke. Indeed, she herself had never been driven or scolded. Her father had always reasoned with her. Doctors and nurses had always reasoned with her. Even Granny had always reasoned with her. So, now, she thought very carefully before she spoke again. But she kept her eyes fixed on Arthur. His eyes did not move from hers but, in some curious way, she knew that he was uneasy.

"I can't prove it," she said at last, "and I hadn't any idea of trying to. I'm only warning you that you must not come in here if you're not to be trusted. And I told you the truth when I said I would rather give you anything in the shop than have you steal it. For I think you must need those things very badly to be willing to get them that way. I don't believe anybody *wants* to steal. Now when you want anything so bad as that, come to me and I'll see if I can get it for you."

Arthur stared at her as if he had not a word on his tongue. "If you think you can frighten me,--" he said. Then, without ending his sentence, he swaggered out of the shop. But to Maida his swagger seemed like something put on to conceal another feeling.

Maida suddenly felt very tired. She wished that Granny Flynn would come back. She wanted Granny to take her into her lap, to cuddle her, to tell her some merry little tale of the Irish fairies. But, instead, the bell rang and another customer came in. While she was waiting on her, Maida noticed somebody come stealthily up to the window, look in and then duck down. She wondered if it might be Billy playing one of his games on her.

The customer went out. In a few moments the bell tinkled again. Maida had been leaning against the counter, her tired head on her outstretched arms. She looked up. It was Arthur Duncan.

He strode straight over to her.

"Here's three cents for your rubber," he said, "and five for your pencil, five for the blank book and there's two dimes I took out of the money-drawer."

Maida did not know what to say. The tears came to her eyes and rolled down her cheeks. Arthur shifted his weight from one foot to the other in intense embarrassment.

"I didn't know it would make you feel as bad as that," he said.

"I don't feel bad," Maida sobbed--and to prove it she smiled while the tears ran down her cheeks--"I feel glad."

What he would have answered to this she never knew. For at that moment the door flew open. The little rowdy boys who had been troubling her so much lately, let out a series of blood-curdling yells.

"What's that?" Arthur asked.

"I don't know who they are," Maida said wearily, "but they do that three or four times every night. I don't know what to do about it."

"Well, I do," Arthur said. "You wait!"

He went over to the door and waited, flattening himself against the wall. After a long silence, they could hear footsteps tip-toeing on the bricks outside. The door flew open. Arthur Duncan leaped like a cat through the opening. There came back to Maida the sound of running, then a pause, then another sound very much as if two or three naughty little heads were being vigorously knocked together. She heard Arthur say:

"Let me catch one of you doing that again and I'll lick you till you can't stand up. And remember I'll be watching for you every night now."

Maida did not see him again then. But just before dinner the bell rang. When Maida opened the door there stood Arthur.

"I had this kitten and I thought you might like him," he said awkwardly, holding out a little bundle of gray fluff.

"Want it!" Maida said. She seized it eagerly. "Oh, thank you, Arthur, ever so much. Oh, Granny, look at this darling kit-kat. What a ball of fluff he is! I'll call him Fluff. And he isn't an Angora or a prize kitty of any kind--just a beautiful plain everyday cat--the kind I've always wanted!"

Even this was not all. After dinner the shop bell rang again. This time it was Arthur and Rosie. Rosie's lips were very tight as if she had made up her mind to some bold deed but her flashing eyes showed her excitement.

"Can we see you alone for a moment, Maida?" she asked in her most business-like tones.

Wondering, Maida shut the door to the living-room and came back to them.

"Maida," Rosie began, "Arthur told me all about the rubber and the pencil and the blank book and the dimes. Of course, I felt pretty bad when I heard about it. But I wanted Arthur to come right over here and explain the whole thing to you. You see Arthur took those things to give away to Dicky because Dicky has such a hard time getting anything he wants."

"Yes, I saw them over at Dicky's," Maida said.

"And then, there was a great deal more to it that Arthur's just told me and I thought you ought to know it at once. You see Arthur's father belongs to a club that meets once a month and Arthur goes there a lot with him. And those men think that plenty of people have things that they have no right to--oh, like automobiles--I mean, things that they haven't earned. And the men in Mr. Duncan's club say that it's perfectly right to take things away from people who have too much and give them to people who have too little. But I say that may be all right for grown people but when children do it, it's just plain *stealing*. And that's all there is to it! But I wanted you to know that Arthur thought it was right--well sort of right, you understand--when he took those things. You don't think so now, do you, after the talking-to I've given you?" She turned severely on Arthur.

Arthur shuffled and looked embarrassed. "No," he said sheepishly, "not until you're grown up."

"But what I wanted to say next, Maida," Rosie continued, "is, please not to tell Dicky. He would be so surprised--and then he wouldn't keep the things that Arthur gave him. And of course now that Arthur has paid for them--they're all right for him to have."

"Of course I wouldn't tell anybody," Maida said in a shocked voice, "not even Granny or Billy--not even my father."

"Then that's settled," Rosie said with a sigh. "Good night."

The next day the following note reached Maida:

You are cordully invited to join the W.M.N.T. Club which meets
three times a week at the house of Miss Rosie Brine, or Mr.
Richard Dore or Mr. Arthur Duncan.

P.S. The name means, WE MUST NEVER TELL.

Maida dreamed nothing but happy dreams that night.

CHAPTER VIII: A RAINY DAY

The next day it rained dismally. Maida had been running the shop for three weeks but this was her first experience with stormy weather. Because she, herself, had never been allowed to set her foot outdoors when the weather was damp, she expected that she would see no children that day. But long before the bell rang they crowded in wet streaming groups into the shop. And at nine the lines disappearing into the big school doorways seemed as long as ever.

Even the Clark twins in rubber boots, long rain-capes and a baby umbrella came in to spend their daily pennies.

"I guess it'll be one session, Maida," Dorothy whispered.

"Oh goody, Dorothy!" Mabel lisped. "Don't you love one session, Maida?"

Maida was ashamed to confess to two such tiny girls that she did not know what "one session" meant. But she puzzled over it the whole morning. If Rosie and Arthur had come in she would have asked them. But neither of them appeared. Indeed, they were not anywhere in the lines--Maida looked very carefully.

At twelve o'clock the school bell did not ring. In surprise, Maida craned out of the window to consult the big church clock. It agreed exactly with the tall grandfather's clock in the living-room. Both pointed to twelve, then to five minutes after and ten and fifteen--still no bell.

A little later Dicky came swinging along, the sides of his old rusty raincoat flapping like the wings of some great bird.

"It's one-session, Maida," he said jubilantly, "did you hear the bell?"

"What's one session, Dicky?" Maida asked.

"Why, when it's too stormy for the children to go to school in the afternoon the fire-bells ring twenty-two at quarter to twelve. They keep all the classes in until one o'clock though."

"Oh, that's why they don't come out," Maida said.

At one o'clock the umbrellas began to file out of the school door. The street looked as if it had grown a monster crop of shiny black toad-stools. But it was the only sign of life that the neighborhood showed for the rest of the day. The storm was too violent for even the big boys and girls to brave. A very long afternoon went by. Not a customer came into the shop. Maida felt very lonely. She wandered from shop to living-room and from living-room to chamber. She tried to read. She sewed a little. She even popped corn for a lonesome fifteen minutes. But it seemed as if the long dark day would never go.

As they were sitting down to dinner that night, Billy bounced in--his face pink and wet, his eyes sparkling like diamonds from his conflict with the winds.

"Oh, Billy, how glad I am to see you," Maida said. "It's been the lonesomest day."

"Sure, the sight av ye's grand for sore eyes," said Granny.

Maida had noticed that Billy's appearance always made the greatest difference in everything. Before he came, the noise of the wind howling about the store made Maida sad. Now it seemed the jolliest of sounds. And when at seven, Rosie appeared, Maida's cup of happiness brimmed over.

While Billy talked with Granny, the two little girls rearranged the stock.

"My mother was awful mad with me just before supper," Rosie began at once. "It seems as if she was so cross lately that there's no living with her. She picks on me all the time. That's why I'm here. She sent me to bed. But I made up my mind I wouldn't go to bed. I climbed out my bedroom window and came over here."

"Oh, Rosie, I wish you wouldn't do that," Maida said. "Oh, do run right home! Think how worried your mother would be if she went up into your room and found you gone. She wouldn't know what had become of you."

"Well, then, what makes her so strict with me?" Rosie cried. Her eyes had grown as black as thunder clouds. The scowl that made her face so sullen had come deep between her eyebrows.

"Oh, how I wish I had a mother," Maida said longingly. "I guess I wouldn't say a word to her, no matter how strict she was."

"I guess you don't know what you'd do until you tried it," Rosie said.

Granny and Billy had been curiously quiet in the other room. Suddenly Billy

Potter stepped to the door.

"I've just thought of a great game, children," he said. "But we've got to play it in the kitchen. Bring some crayons, Maida."

The children raced after him. "What is it?" they asked in chorus.

Billy did not answer. He lifted Granny's easy-chair with Granny, knitting and all, and placed it in front of the kitchen stove. Then he began to draw a huge rectangle on the clean, stone floor.

"Guess," he said.

"Sure and Oi know what ut's going to be," smiled Granny.

Maida and Rosie watched him closely. Suddenly they both shouted together: "Hopscotch! Hopscotch!"

"Right you are!" Billy approved. He searched among the coals in the hod until he found a hard piece of slate.

"All ready now!" he said briskly. "Your turn, first, Rosie, because you're company."

Rosie failed on "fivesy." Maida's turn came next and she failed on "threesy." Billy followed Maida but he hopped on the line on "twosy."

"Oi belave Oi cud play that game, ould as Oi am," Granny said suddenly.

"I bet you could," Billy said.

"Sure, 'twas a foine player Oi was when Oi was a little colleen."

"Come on, Granny," Billy said.

The two little girls jumped up and down, clapping their hands and shrieking, "Granny's going to play!" "Granny's going to play!" They made so much noise finally, that Billy had to threaten to stand them on their heads in a corner.

Granny took her turn after Billy. She hopped about like a very active and a very benevolent old fairy.

"Oh, doesn't she look like the Dame in fairy tales?" Maida said.

They played for a half an hour. And who do you suppose won? Not Maida with all her new-found strength, not Rosie with all her nervous energy, not Billy with all his athletic training.

"Mrs. Delia Flynn, champion of America and Ireland," Billy greeted the victor. "Granny, we'll have to enter you in the next Olympic games."

They returned after this breathless work to the living-room.

"Now I'm going to tell you a story," Billy announced.

"Oh! Oh! Oh!" Maida squealed. "Do! Billy tells the most wonderful stories, Rosie--stories he's heard and stories he's read. But the most wonderful ones are those that he makes up as he goes along."

The two little girls settled themselves on the hearth-rug at Billy's feet. Granny sat, not far off, working with double speed at her neglected knitting.

"Once upon a time," Billy said, "there lived a little girl named Klara. And Klara was the naughtiest little girl in the world. She was a pretty child and a clever child and everybody would have loved her if she had only given them a chance. But how can you love a child who is doing naughty things all the time? Particularly was she a great trial to her mother. That poor lady was not well and needed care and attention, herself. But instead of giving her these, Klara gave her only hard words and disobedient acts. The mother used sometimes to punish her little daughter but it seemed as if this only made her worse. Both father and mother were in despair about her. Klara seemed to be growing steadily worse and worse. And, indeed, lately, she had added to her naughtiness by threatening to run away.

"One night, it happened, Klara had been so bad that her mother had put her to bed early. The moment her mother left the room, Klara whipped over to the window. 'I'm going to dress myself and climb out the window and run away and never come back,' she said to herself.'

"The house in which Klara lived was built on the side of a cliff, overlooking the sea. As Klara stood there in her nightgown the moon began to rise and come up out of the water. Now the moonrise is always a beautiful sight and Klara stopped for a moment to watch it, fascinated.

"It seemed to her that she had never seen the moon look so big before. And certainly she had never seen it such a color--a soft deep orange. In fact, it might have been an immense orange--or better, a monster pumpkin stuck on the horizon-line.

"The strange thing about the moon, though, was that it grew larger instead of smaller. It rose higher and higher, growing bigger and bigger, until it was half-way up the curve of the sky. Then it stopped short. Klara watched it, her eyes bulging out of her head. In all her experience she had never seen such a surprising thing. And while she watched, another remarkable thing happened. A great door in the moon opened suddenly and there on the threshold stood a little old lady. A strange little old lady she was--a little old lady with short red skirts and high, gayly-flowered draperies at her waist, a little old lady with a tall black, sugar-loaf hat, a great white ruff around her neck and little red shoes with bright silver buckles on them--a little old lady who carried a black cat perched on one shoulder and a broomstick in one hand.

"The little old lady stooped down and lifted something over the threshold. Klara strained her eyes to see what it was. It looked like a great roll of golden carpeting. With a sudden deft movement the little old lady threw it out of the door. It flew straight across the ocean, unrolling as swiftly as a ball of twine that you've flung across the room. It came nearer and nearer. The farther it got from the moon, the faster it unrolled. After a while it struck against the shore right under Klara's window and Klara saw that it was the wake of the moon. She watched.

"The little old lady had disappeared from the doorway in the moon but the door did not close. And, suddenly, still another wonderful thing happened. The golden wake lifted itself gradually from the water until it was on a level with Klara's window. Bending down she touched it with both her soft little hands. It was as firm and hard as if it had been woven from strands of gold.

"'Now's my time to run away from my cross mother,' Klara said to herself. 'I guess that nice old lady in the moon wants me to come and be her little girl. Well, I'll go. I guess they'll be sorry in this house to-morrow when they wake up and find they're never going to see me again.'

"Opening the window gently that nobody might hear her, she stepped on to the Wake of Gold. It felt cool and hard to her little bare feet. It inclined gently from her window. She ran down the slope until she reached the edge of the sea. There she hesitated. For a moment it seemed a daring thing to walk straight out to the moon with nothing between her and the water but a path of gold. Then she recalled how her mother had sent her to bed and her heart hardened. She started briskly out.

"From Klara's window it had looked as though it would take her only a few moments to get to the moon. But the farther she went, the farther from her the doorway seemed to go. But she did not mind that the walk was so long because it was so pretty. Looking over the edge of the Wake of Gold, deep down in the water, she could see all kinds of strange sights.

"At one place a school of little fish swam up to the surface of the water. Klara knelt down and watched their pretty, graceful motions. The longer she gazed the more fish she saw and the more beautiful they seemed. Pale-blue fishes with silver spots. Pale-pink ones with golden stripes. Gorgeous red ones with jewelled black horns. Brilliant yellow and green ones that shone like phosphorus. And here and there, gliding among them, were what seemed little angel-fish like living rainbows, whose filmy wing-like fins changed color when they swam.

"Klara reached into the water and tried to catch some of these marvelous beings.

"But at her first motion--bing! The water looked as if it were streaked with rainbow lightning. Swish! It was dull and clear again, with nothing between her and the quiet, seaweed-covered bottom.

"A little farther along Klara came across a wonderful sea-grotto. Again she knelt down on the Wake of Gold and watched. At the bottom the sand was so white and shiny that it might have been made of star-dust. Growing up from it were beds of marvelous seaflowers, opening and shutting delicate petals, beautiful seafans that waved with every ripple, high, thick shrubs and towering trees in which the fishes had built their nests. In and out among all this undergrowth, frisked tiny sea-horses, ridden by mischievous sea-urchins. They leaped and trotted and galloped as if they were so happy that they did not know what to do. Klara felt that she must play with them. She put one little foot into the water to attract their attention. Bing! The water seemed alive with scuttling things. Swish! The grotto was so quiet that she could not believe that there was anything living in it.

"A little farther on, Klara came upon a sight even more wonderful than this--a village of mer-people. It was set so far down in the water that it seemed a million miles away. And yet the water was so clear that she felt she could touch the house-tops.

"The mer-houses seemed to be made of a beautiful, sparkling white coral with big, wide-open windows through which the tide drifted. The mer-streets seemed to be cobbled in pearl, the sidewalks to be paved in gold. At their sides grew mer-trees, the highest she had ever seen, with all kinds of beautiful singing fish roosting in their branches. Little mer-boats of carved pink coral with purple seaweed sails or of mother-of-pearl with rosy, mer-flower-petal sails, were floating through the streets. In some, sat little mer-maidens, the sunlight flashing on their pretty green scales, on their long, golden tresses, on the bright mirrors they held in their hands. Other boats held little mer-boys who made beautiful music on the harps they carried.

"At one end of the mer-village Klara could see one palace, bigger and more beautiful than all the others. Through an open window she caught a glimpse of the mer-king--a jolly old fellow with a fat red face and a long white beard sitting on a throne of gold. At his side reclined the mer-queen--a very beautiful lady with a skin as white as milk and eyes as green as emeralds. Little mer-princes and little mer-princesses were playing on the floor with tiny mer-kittens and tinier mer-puppies. One sweet little mer-baby was tiptailing towards the window with a pearl that she had stolen from her sister's coronet.

"It seemed to Klara that this mer-village was the most enchanting place that she had ever seen in her life. Oh, how she wanted to live there!

"'Oh, good mer-king,' she called entreatingly, 'and good mer-queen, please let me come to live in your palace.'

"Bing! The water rustled and roiled as if all the birds of paradise that the world contained had taken flight. Swish! It was perfectly quiet again. The mer-village was as deserted as a graveyard.

"'Well, if they don't want me, they shan't get me, Klara said. And she walked on twice as proud.'

"By this time she was getting closer and closer to the moon. The nearer she came the bigger it grew. Now it filled the entire sky. The door had remained open all this time. Through it she could see a garden--a garden more beautiful than any fairy-tale garden that she had ever read about. From the doorway silvery paths stretched between hedges as high as a giant's head. Sometimes these paths ended in fountains whose spray twisted into all kinds of fairy-like shapes. Sometimes these paths seemed to stop flush against the clouds. Nearer stretched flower-beds so brilliant that you would have thought a kaleidoscope had broken on the ground. Birds, like living jewels, flew in and out through the tree-branches. They sang so hard that it seemed to Klara they must burst their little throats. From the branches hung all kinds of precious stones, all kinds of delicious-looking fruits and candies.

"Klara could not scramble through the door quickly enough.

"But as she put one foot on the threshold the little old lady appeared. She looked as if she had stepped out of a fairy-tale. And yet Klara had a strange feeling of discomfort when she looked at her. It seemed to Klara that the old lady's mouth was cruel and her eyes hard.

"'Are you the little girl who's run away?' the old lady asked.

"'Yes,' Klara faltered.

"'And you want to live in the Kingdom of the Moon?'

"'Yes.'

"'Enter then.'

"The old lady stepped aside and Klara marched across the threshold. She felt the door swinging to behind her. She heard a bang as it closed, shutting her out of the world and into the moon.

"And then--and then--what do you think happened?"

Billy stopped for a moment. Rosie and Maida rose to their knees.

"What happened?" they asked breathlessly.

"The garden vanished as utterly as if it were a broken soap-bubble. Gone were the trees and the flowers; gone were the fountains and the birds; gone, too, were the jewels, the candies and the fruits.

"The place had become a huge, dreary waste, stretching as far as Klara could see into the distance. It seemed to her as if all the trash that the world had outgrown had been dumped here--it was so covered with heaps of old rubbish.

"Klara turned to the old lady. She had not changed except that her cruel mouth sneered.

"Klara burst into tears. 'I want to go home,' she screamed. 'Let me go back to my mother.'

"The old lady only smiled. 'You open that door and let me go back to my mother,' Klara cried passionately.

"'But I can't open it,' the old lady said. 'It's locked. I have no keys.'

"'Where are the keys?' Klara asked.

"The old lady pointed to the endless heaps of rubbish. 'There, somewhere,' she said.

"'I'll find them,' Klara screamed, 'and open that door and run back to my home. You shan't keep me from my own dear mother, you wicked woman.'

"'Nobody wants to keep you,' the old lady said. 'You came of your own accord. Find the keys if you want to go back.'

"That was true and Klara wisely did not answer. But you can fancy how she regretted coming. She began to search among the dump-heaps. She could find no keys. But the longer she hunted the more determined she grew. It seemed to her that she searched for weeks and weeks.

"It was very discouraging, very dirty and very fatiguing work. She moved always in a cloud of dust. At times it seemed as if her back would break from bending so much. Often she had to bite her lips to keep from screaming with rage after she had gone through a rubbish-pile as high as her head and, still, no keys. All kinds of venomous insects stung her. All kinds of vines and brambles scratched her. All kinds of stickers and thistles pricked her. Her little feet and hands bled all the time. But still she kept at it. After that first conversation, Klara never spoke with the old lady again. After a few days Klara left her in the distance. At the end of a week, the moon-door was no longer in sight when Klara looked back.

"But during all those weeks of weary work Klara had a chance to think. She saw for the first time what a naughty little girl she had been and how she had worried the kindest mother in the world. Her longing for her mother grew so great at times that she had to sit down and cry. But after a while she would dry her eyes and go at the hunt with fresh determination.

"One day she caught a glint of something shining from a clump of bushes. She had to dig and dig to get at it for about these bushes the ashes were packed down hard. But finally she uncovered a pair of iron keys. On one was printed in letters of gold, 'I'M SORRY,' on the other, 'I'LL NEVER DO SO AGAIN.'

"Klara seized the keys joyfully and ran all the long way back to the great door. It had two locks. She put one key in the upper lock, turned it--a great bolt jarred. She put the other key into the second lock, turned it--a great bolt jarred. The door swung open.

"'I'm sorry,' Klara whispered to herself. 'I'll never do so again.'

"She had a feeling that as long as she said those magic words, everything would go well with her.

"Extending out from the door was the Wake of Gold. Klara bounded through the opening and ran. She turned back after a few moments and there was the old lady with her cat and her broomstick standing in the doorway. But the old lady's face had grown very gentle and kind.

"Klara did not look long. She ran as fast as she could pelt across the golden path, whispering, 'I'm sorry. I will never do so again. I'm sorry. I will never do so again. I'm sorry. I will never do so again.'

"And as she ran all the little mer-people came to the surface of the water to encourage her. The little mer-maidens flashed their mirrors at her. The little mer-boys played wonderful music on their harps. The mer-king gave her a jolly smile and the mer-queen blew her a kiss. All the little mer-princesses and all the little mer-princes held up their pets to her. Even the mer-baby clapped her dimpled hands.

"And farther on all the little sea horses with the sea urchins on their backs assembled in bobbing groups. And farther on all the little rainbow fishes gathered in shining files. As she ran all the scratches and gashes in her flesh healed up.

"After a while she reached her own window. Opening it, she jumped in. Turning to pull it down she saw the old lady disappear from the doorway of the moon, saw the door close upon her, saw the Wake of Gold melt and fall into the sea where it lay in a million gleaming spangles, saw the moon float up into the sky, growing smaller and smaller and paler and paler until it was no larger than a silver plate. And now it was the moon no longer--it was the sun. Its rays were shining hot on her face. She was back in her little bed. Her mother's arms were about her and Klara was saying, 'I'm SORRY. I WILL NEVER DO SO AGAIN.'"

For a long time after Billy finished the room was very quiet. Then suddenly Rosie jumped to her feet. "That was a lovely story, Billy," she said. "But I guess I don't want to hear any more now. I think I'll go home."

CHAPTER IX: WORK

It was still raining when Maida got up the next day. It rained all the morning. She listened carefully at a quarter to twelve for the one-session bell but it did not ring. Just before school began in the afternoon Rosie came into the shop. Maida saw at once that something had happened to her. Rosie's face looked strange and she dragged across the room instead of pattering with her usual quick, light step.

"What do you think's happened, Maida?" Rosie asked.

"I don't know. Oh, what?" Maida asked affrighted.

"When I came home from school this noon mother wasn't there. But Aunt Theresa was there--she'd cooked the dinner. She said that mother had gone away for a visit and that she wouldn't be back for some time. She said she was going to keep house for father and me while mother was gone. I feel dreadfully homesick and lonesome without mother."

"Oh Rosie, I am sorry," Maida said. "But perhaps your mother won't stay long. Do you like your Aunt Theresa?"

"Oh, yes, I like her. But of course she isn't mother."

"No, of course. Nobody is like your mother."

"Oh, yes; there's something else I had to tell you. The W.M.N.T.'s are going to meet at Dicky's after school this afternoon. Be sure to come, Maida."

"Of course I'll come." Maida's whole face sparkled. "That is, if Granny doesn't think it's too wet."

Rosie lingered for a few moments but she did not seem like her usual happy-go-lucky self. And when she left, Maida noticed that instead of running across the street she actually walked.

All the morning long Maida talked of nothing to Granny but the prospective meeting of the W.M.N.T.'s. "Just think, Granny, I never belonged to a club before," she said again and again.

Very early she had put out on her bed the clothes that she intended to wear--a tanbrown serge of which she was particularly fond, and her favorite "tire" of a delicate, soft lawn. She kept rushing to the window to study the sky. It continued to look like the inside of a dull tin cup. She would not have eaten any lunch at all if Granny had not told her that she must. And her heart sank steadily all the afternoon for the rain continued to come down.

"I don't suppose I can go, Granny," she faltered when the clock struck four.

"Sure an you *can*," Granny responded briskly.

But she wrapped Maida up, as Maida herself said: "As if I was one of papa's carved crystals come all the way from China."

First Granny put on a sweater, then a coat, then over all a raincoat. She put a hood on her head and a veil over that. She made her wear rubber boots and take an umbrella. Maida got into a gale of laughter during the dressing.

"I ought to be wrapped in excelsior now," she said. "If I fall down in the puddle in the court, Granny," she threatened merrily, "I never can pick myself up. I'll either have to roll and roll and roll until I get on to dry land or I'll have to wait until somebody comes and shovels me out."

But she did not fall into the puddle. She walked carefully along the edge and then ran as swiftly as her clothes and lameness would permit. She arrived in Dicky's garret, red-cheeked and breathless.

Arthur and Rosie had already come. Rosie was playing on the floor with Delia and the puppy that she had rescued from the tin-can persecution. Rosie was growling, the dog was yelping and Delia was squealing--but all three with delight.

Arthur and Dicky sat opposite each other, working at the round table.

"What do you think of that dog now, Maida?" Rosie asked proudly. "His name is 'Tag.' You wouldn't know him for the same dog, would you? Isn't he a nice-looking little puppy?"

Tag did look like another dog. He wore a collar and his yellowy coat shone like satin. His whole manner had changed. He came running over to Maida and stood looking at her with the most spirited air in the world, his head on one side, one paw up and one ear cocked inquisitively. His tail wriggled so fast that Delia thinking it some wonderful new toy, kept trying to catch it and hold it in her little fingers.

"He's a lovely doggie," Maida said. "I wish I'd brought Fluff."

"And did you ever see such a dear baby," Rosie went on, hugging Delia. "Oh, if I only had a baby brother or sister!"

"She's a darling," Maida agreed heartily. "Babies are so much more fun than dolls, don't you think so, Rosie?"

"Dolls!" No words can express the contempt that was in Miss Brine's accent.

"What are you doing, Dicky?" Maida asked, limping over to the table.

"Making things," Dicky said cheerfully.

On the table were piles of mysterious-looking objects made entirely of paper. Some were of white paper and others of brown, but they were all decorated with trimmings of colored tissue.

"What are they?" Maida asked. "Aren't they lovely? I never saw anything like them in my life."

Dicky blushed all over his face at this compliment but it was evident that he was delighted. "Well, those are paper-boxes," he said, pointing to the different piles of things, "and those are steamships. Those are the old-fashioned kind with double smokestacks. Those are double-boats, jackets, pants, badges, nose-pinchers, lamp-lighters, firemen's caps and soldier caps."

"Oh, that's why you buy all that colored paper," Maida said in a tone of great satisfaction. "I've often wondered." She examined Dicky's work carefully. She could see that it was done with remarkable precision and skill. "Oh, what fun to do things like that. I do wish you'd show me how to make them, Dicky. I'm such a useless girl. I can't make a single thing."

"I'll show you, sure," Dicky offered generously.

"What are you making so many for?" Maida queried.

"Well, you see it's this way," Dicky began in a business-like air. "Arthur and Rosie and I are going to have a fair. We've had a fair every spring and every fall for the last three years. That's how we get our money for Christmas and the Fourth of July. Arthur whittles things out of wood--he'll show you what he can do in a minute--he's a crackajack. Rosie makes candy. And I make these paper things."

"And do you make much money?" Maida asked, deeply interested.

"Don't make any money at all," Dicky said. "The children pay us in nails. I charge them ten nails a-piece for the easy things and twenty nails for the hardest. Arthur can get more for his stuff because it's harder to do."

"But what do you want nails for?" Maida asked in bewilderment.

"Why, nails are junk."

"And what's junk?"

The three children stared at her. "Don't you know what *junk* is, Maida?" Rosie asked in despair.

"No."

"Junk's old iron," Dicky explained. "And you sell it to the junkman. Once we made forty cents out of one of these fairs. One reason we're beginning so early this year, I've got something very particular I want to buy my mother for a Christmas present. Can you keep a secret, Maida?"

Maida nodded.

"Well, it's a fur collar for her neck. They have them down in a store on Main street every winter--two dollars and ninetyeight cents. It seems an awful lot but I've got over a dollar saved up. And I guess I can do it if I work hard."

"How much have you made ordinarily?" Maida asked thoughtfully.

"Once we made forty cents a-piece but that's the most."

"I tell you what you do," Maida burst out impetuously after a moment of silence in which she considered this statement. "When the time comes for you to hold your fair, I'll lend you my shop for a day. I'll take all the things out of the window and I'll clean all the shelves off and you boys can put your things there. I'll clear out the showcases for Rosie's candy. Won't that be lovely?" She smiled happily.

"It would be grand business for us," Dicky said soberly, "but somehow it doesn't seem quite fair to you."

"Oh, please don't think of that," Maida said. "I'd just love to do it. And you must teach me how to make things so that I can help you. You will take the shop, Dicky?" she pleaded. "And you, Rosie? And Arthur?" She looked from one to the other with all her heart in her eyes.

But nobody spoke for a moment. "It seems somehow as if we oughtn't to," Dicky said awkwardly at last.

Maida's lip trembled. At first she could not understand. Here she was aching to do a kindness to these three friends of hers. And they, for some unknown reason, would not permit it. It was not that they disliked her, she knew. What was it? She tried to put herself in their place. Suddenly it came to her what the difficulty was. They did not want to be so much in her debt. How could she prevent that? She must let them do something for her that would lessen that debt. But what? She thought very hard. In a flash it came to her--a plan by which she could make it all right.

"You see," she began eagerly, "I wanted to ask you three to help me in something, but I can't do it unless you let me help you. Listen--the next holiday is Halloween. I want to decorate my shop with a lot of real jack-o'-lanterns cut from pumpkins. It will be hard work and a lot of it and I was hoping that perhaps you'd help me with this."

The three faces lighted up.

"Of course we will," Dicky said heartily.

"Gee, I bet Dicky and I could make some great lanterns," Arthur said reflectively.

"And I'll help you fix up the store," Rosie said with enthusiasm. "I just love to make things look pretty."

"It's a bargain then," Maida said. "And now you must teach me how to help you this very afternoon, Dicky."

They fell to work with a vim. At least three of them did. Rosie continued to frisk with Delia and Tag on the floor. Dicky started Maida on the caps first. He said that those were the easiest. And, indeed she had very little trouble with anything until she came to the boxes. She had to do her first box over and over again before it would come right. But Dicky was very patient with her. He kept telling her that she did better than most beginners or she would have given it up. When she made her first good box, her face beamed with satisfaction.

"Do you mind if I take it home, Dicky?" she asked. "I'd like to show it to my father when he comes. It's the first thing I ever made in my life."

"Of course," Dicky said.

"Don't the other children ever try to copy your things?" Maida asked.

"They try to," Arthur answered, "but they never do so well as Dicky."

"You ought to see their nose-pinchers," Rosie laughed. "They can't stand up straight. And their boxes and steamships are the wobbliest things."

"I'm going to get all kinds of stuff for things we make for the fair," Maida said reflectively. "Gold and silver paper and colored stars and pretty fancy pictures for trimmings. You see if you're going to charge real money you must make them more beautiful than those for which you only charged nails."

"That's right," Dicky said. "By George, that will be great! You go ahead and buy whatever you think is right, Maida, and I'll pay you for it from what we take in at the fair."

"That's settled. What do you whittle, Arthur?"

"Oh, all kinds of things--things I made up myself and things I learned how to do in sloyd in school. I make bread-boards and rolling pins and shinny sticks and cats and little baskets out of cherry-stones."

"Jiminy crickets, he's forgetting the boats," Dicky burst in enthusiastically. "He makes the dandiest boats you ever saw in your life."

Maida looked at Arthur in awe. "I never heard anything like it! Can you make anything for girls?"

"Made me a set of the darlingest dolls' furniture you ever saw in your life," Rosie put in from the floor.

"Say, did you get into any trouble last night?" Arthur turned suddenly to Rosie. "I forgot to ask you."

"Arthur and Rosie hooked jack yesterday, in all that rain," Dicky explained to Maida. "They knew a place where they could get a whole lot of old iron and they were afraid if they waited, it would be gone."

"I should say I did," Rosie answered Arthur's question. "Somebody went and tattled to my mother. Of course, I was wet through to the skin and that gave the whole thing away, anyway. I got the worst scolding and mother sent me to bed without my supper. But I climbed out the window and went over to see Maida. I don't mind! I hate school and as long as I live I shall never go except when I want to--never, never, never! I guess I'm not going to be shut up studying when I'd rather be out in the open air. Wouldn't you hook jack if you wanted to, Maida?"

Maida did not reply for an instant. She hated to have Rosie ask this question, point-blank for she did not want to answer it. If she said exactly what she thought there might be trouble. And it seemed to her that she would do almost anything rather than lose Rosie's friendship. But Maida had been taught to believe that the truth is the most precious thing in the world. And so she told the truth after a while but it was with a great effort.

"No, I wouldn't," she said.

"Oh, that's all right for *you* to say," Rosie said firing up. "You don't have to go to school. You live the easiest life that anybody can--just sitting in a chair and tending shop all day. What do you know about it, anyway?"

Maida's lips quivered. "It is true I don't go to school, Rosie," she said. "But it isn't because I don't want to. I'd give anything on earth if I could go. I watch that line of children every morning and afternoon of my life and wish and *wish* and WISH I was in it. And when the windows are opened and I hear the singing and reading, it seems as if I just couldn't stand it."

"Oh, well," Rosie's tone was still scornful. "I don't believe, even if you did go to school, that you'd ever do anything bad. You'd never be anything but a fraid-cat and teacher's pet."

"I guess I'd be so glad to be there, I'd do anything the teacher asked," Maida said dejectedly. "I do a lot of things that bother Granny but I guess I never have been a very naughty girl. You can't be very naughty with your leg all crooked under you." Maida's voice had grown bitter. The children looked at her in amazement. "But what's the use of talking to you two," she went on. "You could never understand. I guess Dicky knows what I mean, though."

To their great surprise, Maida put her head down on the table and cried.

For a moment the room was perfectly silent. The fire snapped and Dicky went over to look at it. He stood with his back turned to the other children but a suspicious snuffle came from his direction. Arthur Duncan walked to the window and stood looking out. Rosie sat still, her eyes downcast, her little white teeth biting her red lips. Then suddenly she jumped to her feet, ran like a whirlwind to Maida's side. She put her arms about the bowed figure.

"Oh, do excuse me, Maida," she begged. "I know I'm the worst girl in the world. Everybody says so and I guess it's true. But I do love you and I wouldn't have hurt your feelings for anything. I don't believe you'd be a fraid-cat or teacher's pet--I truly don't. Please excuse me."

Maida wiped her tears away. "Of course I'll excuse you! But just the same, Rosie, I hope you won't hook jack any more for someday you'll be sorry."

"I'm going to make some candy now," Rosie said, adroitly changing the subject.

"I brought some molasses and butter and everything I need." She began to bustle about the stove. Soon they were all laughing again.

Maida had never pulled candy before and she thought it the most enchanting fun in the world. It was hard to keep at work, though, when it was such a temptation to stop and eat it. But she persevered and succeeded in pulling hers whiter than anybody's. She laughed and talked so busily that, when she started to put on her things, all traces of tears had disappeared.

The rain had stopped. The puddle was of monster size after so long a storm. They came out just in time to help Molly fish Tim out of the water and to prevent Betsy from giving a stray kitten a bath. Following Rosie and Arthur, Maida waded through it from one end to the other--it seemed the most perilous of adventures to her.

After that meeting, the W.M.N.T.'s were busier than they had ever been. Every other afternoon, and always when it was bad weather, they worked at Maida's house. Granny gave Maida a closet all to herself and as fast as the things were finished they were put in boxes and stowed away on its capacious shelves.

Arthur whittled and carved industriously. His work went slower than Dicky's of course but, still, it went with remarkable quickness. Maida often stopped her own work on the paper things to watch Arthur's. It was a constant marvel to her that such big, awkward-looking hands could perform feats of such delicacy. Her own fingers, small and delicate as they were, bungled surprisingly at times.

"And as for the paste," Maida said in disgust to Rosie one day, "you'd think that I fell into the paste-pot every day. I wash it off my hands and face. I pick it off of my clothes and sometimes Granny combs it out of my hair."

Often after dinner, the W.M.N.T.'s would call in a body on Maida. Then would follow long hours of such fun that Maida hated to hear the clock strike nine. Always there would be molasses-candy making by the capable Rosie at the kitchen stove and corn-popping by the vigorous Arthur on the living-room hearth. After the candy had cooled and the pop corn had been flooded in melted butter, they would gather about the hearth to roast apples and chestnuts and to listen to the fairy-tales that Maida would read.

The one thing which she could do and they could not was to read with the ease and expression of a grown person. As many of her books were in French as in

English and it was the wonder of the other W.M.N.T.'s that she could read a French story, translating as she went. Her books were a delight to Arthur and Dicky and she lent them freely. Rosie liked to listen to stories but she did not care to read.

Maida was very happy nowadays. Laura was the only person in the Court who had caused her any uneasiness. Since the day that Laura had made herself so disagreeable, Maida had avoided her steadily. Best of all, perhaps, Maida's health had improved so much that even her limp was slowly disappearing.

In the course of time, the children taught Maida the secret language of the W.M.N.T.'s. They could hold long conversations that were unintelligible to anybody else. When at first they used it in fun before Maida, she could not understand a word. After they had explained it to her, she wondered that she had ever been puzzled.

"It's as easy as anything," Rosy said. "You take off the first sound of a word and put it on the end with an *ay* added to it like MAN--an-may. BOY--oy-bay. GIRL--irl-gay. When a word is just one sound like I or O, or when it begins with a vowel like EEL or US or OUT, you add *way*, like I--I-way. O--O-way. EEL--eel-way. US--us-way. OUT--out-way."

Thus Maida could say to Rosie:

"Are-way ou-yay oing-gay o-tay ool-schay o-tay ay-day?" and mean simply, "Are you going to school to-day?"

And sometimes to Maida's grief, Rosie would reply roguishly:

"O-nay I-way am-way oing-gay o-tay ook-hay ack-jay ith-way Arthur-way."

Billy Potter was finally invited to join the W.M.N.T.'s too. He never missed a meeting if he could possibly help it.

"Why do you call Maida, 'Petronilla'?" Dicky asked him curiously one day when Maida had run home for more paper.

"Petronilla is the name of a little girl in a fairy-tale that I read when I was a little boy," Billy answered.

"And was she like Maida?" Arthur asked.

"Very."

"How?" Rosie inquired.

"Petronilla had a gold star set in her forehead by a fairy when she was a baby," Billy explained. "It was a magic star. Nobody but fairies could see it but it was always there. Anybody who came within the light of Petronilla's star, no matter how wicked or hopeless or unhappy he was, was made better and hopefuller and happier."

Nobody spoke for an instant.

Then, "I guess Maida's got the star all right," Dicky said.

Billy was very interested in the secret language. At first when they talked this gibberish before him, he listened mystified. But to their great surprise he never asked a question. They went right on talking as if he were not present. In an interval of silence, Billy said softly:

"I-way onder-way if-way I-way ought-bay a-way uart-quay of-way ice-way-eam-cray, ese-thay ildren-chay ould-way eat-way it-way."

For a moment nobody could speak. Then a deafening, "es-yay!" was shouted at the top of four pairs of lungs.

CHAPTER X: PLAY

But although the W.M.N.T.'s worked very hard, you must not suppose that they left no time to play. Indeed, the weather was so fine that it was hard to stay in the house. The beautiful Indian summer had come and each new day dawned more perfect than the last. The trees had become so gorgeous that it was as if the streets were lined with burning torches. Whenever a breeze came, they seemed to flicker and flame and flare. Maida and Rosie used to shuffle along the gutters gathering pocketsful of glossy horse-chestnuts and handfuls of gorgeous leaves.

Sometimes it seemed to Maida that she did not need to play, that there was fun enough in just being out-of-doors. But she did play a great deal for she was well enough to join in all the fun now and it seemed to her that she never could get enough of any one game.

She would play house and paper-dolls and ring-games with the little children in the morning when the older ones were in school. She would play jackstones with the bigger girls in the afternoon. She would play running games with the crowd of girls and boys, of whom the W.M.N.T.'s were the leaders, towards night. Then sometimes she would grumble to Granny because the days were so short.

Of all the games, Hoist-the-Sail was her favorite. She often served as captain on her side. But whether she called or awaited the cry, "Liberty poles are bending--hoist the sail!" a thrill ran through her that made her blood dance.

"It's no use in talking, Granny," Maida said joyfully one day. "My leg is getting stronger. I jumped twenty jumps to-day without stopping."

After that her progress was rapid. She learned to jump in the rope with Rosie.

They were a pretty sight. People passing often gave them more than one glance--Rosie so vivid and sparkling, in the scarlet cape and hat all velvety jet-blacks, satiny olives and brilliant crimsons--Maida slim, delicate, fairy-like in her long squirrel-coat and cap, her airy ringlets streaming in the breeze and the eyes that had once been so wistful now shining with happiness.

"Do you know what you look like, Maida?" Rosie said once. Before Maida could answer, she went on. "You look like that little mermaid princess in Anderson's fairy tales--the one who had to suffer so to get legs like mortals."

"Do I?" Maida laughed. "Now isn't it strange I have always thought that you look like somebody in a fairy tale, too. You're like Rose-Red in 'Rose-Red and Snow-White.' I think," she added, flushing, for she was a little afraid that it was not polite to say things like this, "that you are the beautifulest girl I ever saw."

"Why, that's just what I think of you," Rosie said in surprise.

"I just love black hair," Maida said.

"And I just adore golden hair," Rosie said. "Now, isn't that strange?"

"I guess," Maida announced after a moment of thought, "people like what they haven't got."

After a while, Rosie taught Maida to jump in the big rope with a half a dozen children at once. Maida never tired of this. When she heard the rope swishing through the air, a kind of excitement came over her. She was proud to think that she had caught the trick--that something inside would warn her when to jump--that she could be sure that this warning would not come an instant too soon or too late. The consciousness of a new strength and a new power made a different child of her. It made her eyes sparkle like gray diamonds. It made her cheeks glow like pink peonies.

By this time she could spin tops with the best of them--sometimes she had five tops going at once. This was a sport of which the W.M.N.T.'s never tired. They kept it up long into the twilight. Sometimes Granny would have to ring the dinner-bell a half a dozen times before Maida appeared. Maida did not mean to be disobedient. She simply did not hear the bell. Granny's scoldings for this carelessness were very gentle--Maida's face was too radiant with her triumph in this new skill.

There was something about Primrose Court--the rows of trees welded into a yellow arch high over their heads, the sky showing through in diamond-shaped glints of blue, the tiny trim houses and their tinier, trimmer yards, the doves pink-toeing everywhere, their throats bubbling color as wonderful as the old Venetian glass in the Beacon Street house, the children running and shouting, the very smell of the dust which their pattering feet threw up--something in the look of all this made Maida's spirits leap.

"I'm happy, ***happy***, HAPPY," Maida said one day. The next--Rosie came rushing into the shop with a frightened face.

"Oh, Maida," she panted, "a terrible thing has happened. Laura Lathrop's got diphtheria--they say she's going to die."

"Oh, Rosie, how dreadful! Who told you so?"

"Annie the cook told Aunt Theresa. Dr. Ames went there three times yesterday. Annie says Mrs. Lathrop looks something awful."

"The poor, poor woman," Granny murmured compassionately.

"Oh, I'm so sorry I was cross to Laura," Maida said, conscience-stricken. "Oh, I do hope she won't die."

"It must be dreadful for Laura," Rosie continued, "Harold can't go near her. Nobody goes into the room but her mother and the nurse."

The news cast a deep gloom over the Court. The little children--Betsy, Molly and Tim played as usual for they could not understand the situation. But the noisy fun of the older children ceased entirely. They gathered on the corner and talked in low voices, watching with dread any movement in the Lathrop house. For a week or more Primrose Court was the quietest spot in the neighborhood.

"They say she's sinking," Rosie said that first night.

The thought of it colored Maida's dreams.

"She's got through the night all right," Rosie reported in the morning, her face shining with hope. "And they think she's a little better." But late the next afternoon, Rosie appeared again, her face dark with dread, "Laura's worse again."

Two or three days passed. Sometimes Laura was better. Oftener she was worse. Dr. Ames's carriage seemed always to be driving into the Court.

"Annie says she's dying," Rosie retailed despairingly. "They don't think she'll live through the night. Oh, won't it be dreadful to wake up to-morrow and find the crape on the door."

The thought of what she might see in the morning kept Maida awake a long time that night. When she arose her first glance was for the Lathrop door. There was no crape.

"No better," Rosie dropped in to say on her way to school "but," she added hopefully, "she's no worse."

Maida watched the Lathrop house all day, dreading to see the undertaker's wagon drive up. But it did not come--not that day, nor the next, nor the next.

"They think she's getting better," Rosie reported joyfully one day.

And gradually Laura did get better. But it was many days before she was well enough to sit up.

"Mrs. Lathrop says," Rosie burst in one day with an excited face, "that if we all gather in front of the house to-morrow at one o'clock, she'll lift Laura up to the window so that we can see her. She says Laura is crazy to see us all."

"Oh, Rosie, I'm so glad!" Maida exclaimed, delighted. Seizing each other by the waist, the two little girls danced about the room.

"Oh, I'm going to be so good to Laura when she gets well," Maida said.

"So am I," Rosie declared with equal fervor. "The last thing I ever said to her was that she was 'a hateful little smarty-cat.'"

Five minutes before one, the next day, all the children in Primrose Court gathered on the lawn in front of Laura's window. Maida led Molly by one hand and Tim by the other. Rosie led Betsy and Delia. Dorothy Clark held Fluff and Mabel held Tag. Promptly at one o'clock, Mrs. Lathrop appeared at the window, carrying a little, thin, white wisp of a girl, all muffled up in a big shawl.

The children broke into shouts of joy. The boys waved their hats and the girls their handkerchiefs. Tag barked madly and Rosie declared afterwards that even Fluff looked excited. But Maida stood still with the tears streaming down her cheeks--Laura's face looked so tiny, her eyes so big and sad. From her own experience, Maida could guess how weak Laura felt.

Laura stayed only an instant at the window. One feeble wave of her claw-like hand and she was gone.

"Annie says Mrs. Lathrop is worn to a shadow trying to find things to entertain Laura," Rosie said one night to Maida and Billy Potter. "She's read all her books to her and played all her games with her and Laura keeps saying she wished she had something new."

"Oh, I do wish we could think of something to do for her," Maida said wistfully. "I know just how she feels. If I could only think of a new toy--but Laura has everything. And then the trouble with toys is that after you've played with them once, there's no more fun in them. I know what that is. If we all had telephones, we could talk to her once in a while. But even that would tire her, I guess."

Billy jumped. "I know what we can do for Laura," he said. "I'll have to have Mrs. Lathrop's permission though." He seized his hat and made for the door. "I'd better see her about it to-night." The door slammed.

It had all happened so suddenly that the children gazed after him with wide-open mouths and eyes.

"What do you suppose it's going to be, Maida?" Rosie asked finally.

"I don't know," Maida answered. "I haven't the least idea. But if Billy makes it, you may be sure it will be wonderful."

When Billy came back, they asked him a hundred questions. But they could not get a word out of him in regard to the new toy.

He appeared at the shop early the next morning with a suit-case full of bundles. Then followed doings that, for a long time, were a mystery to everybody. A crowd of excited children followed him about, asking him dozens of questions and chattering frantically among themselves.

First, he opened one of the bundles--out dropped eight little pulleys. Second, he went up into Maida's bedroom and fastened one of the little pulleys on the sill outside her window. Third, he did the same thing in Rosie's house, in Arthur's and in Dicky's. Fourth, he fastened four of the little pulleys at the playroom window in the Lathrop house.

"Oh, what is he doing?" "I can't think of anything." "Oh, I wish he'd tell us," came from the children who watched these manoeuvres from the street.

Fifth, Billy opened another bundle--this time, out came four coils of a thin rope.

"I know now," Arthur called up to him, "but I won't tell."

Billy grinned.

And, sure enough, "You watch him," was all Arthur would say to the entreaties of his friends.

Sixth, Billy ran a double line of rope between Maida's and Laura's window, a second between Rosie's and Laura's, a third between Arthur's and Laura's, a fourth between Dicky's and Laura's.

Last, Billy opened another bundle. Out dropped four square tin boxes, each with a cover and a handle.

"I've guessed it! I've guessed it!" Maida and Rosie screamed together. "It's a telephone."

"That's the answer," Billy confessed. He went from house to house fastening a box to the lower rope.

"Now when you want to say anything to Laura," he said on his return, "just write a note, put it in the box, pull on the upper string and it will sail over to her window. Suppose you all run home and write something now. I'll go over to Laura's to see how it works."

The children scattered. In a few moments, four excited little faces appeared at as many windows. The telephone worked perfectly. Billy handed Mrs. Lathrop the notes to deliver to Laura.

"Oh, Mr. Potter," Mrs. Lathrop said suddenly, "there's a matter that I wished to speak to you about. That little Flynn girl has lived in the family of Mr. Jerome Westabrook, hasn't she?"

Billy's eyes "skrinkled up." "Yes, Mrs. Lathrop," he admitted, "she lived in the Westabrook family for several years."

"So I guessed," Mrs. Lathrop said. "She's a very sweet little girl," she went on earnestly for she had been touched by the sight of Maida's grief the day that she held Laura to the window. "I hope Mr. Westabrook's own little girl is as sweet."

"She is, Mrs. Lathrop, I assure you she is," Billy said gravely.

"What is the name of the Westabrook child?"

"Elizabeth Fairfax Westabrook."

"What is she like?"

"She's a good deal like Maida," Billy said, his eyes beginning to "skrinkle up" again. "They could easily pass for sisters."

"I suppose that's why the Westabrooks have been so good to the little Flynn girl," Mrs. Lathrop went on, "for they certainly are very good to her. It is quite evident that Maida's clothes belonged once to the little Westabrook girl."

"You are quite right, Mrs. Lathrop. They were made for the little Westabrook girl."

Mrs. Lathrop always declared afterwards that it was the telephone that really cured Laura. Certainly, it proved to be the most exciting of toys to the little invalid. There was always something waiting for her when she waked up in the morning and the tin boxes kept bobbing from window to window until long after dark. The girls kept her informed of what was going on in the neighborhood and the boys sent her jokes and conundrums and puzzle pictures cut from the newspapers. Gifts came to her at all hours. Sometimes it would be a bit of wood-carving--a grotesque face, perhaps--that Arthur had done. Sometimes it was a bit of Dicky's pretty paper-work. Rosie sent her specimens of her cooking from candy to hot roasted potatoes, and Maida sent her daily translations of an exciting fairy tale which she was reading in French for the first time.

Pretty soon Laura was well enough to answer the notes herself. She wrote each of her correspondents a long, grateful and affectionate letter. By and by, she was able to sit in a chair at the window and watch the games. The children remembered every few moments to look and wave to her and she always waved back. At last came the morning when a very thin, pale Laura was wheeled out into the sunshine. After that she grew well by leaps and bounds. In a day or two, she could stand in the ring-games with the little children. By the end of a week, she seemed quite herself.

One morning every child in Primrose Court received a letter in the mail. It was written on gay-tinted paper with a pretty picture at the top. It read:

"You are cordially invited to a Halloween party to be given by
Miss Laura Lathrop at 29 Primrose Court on Saturday evening,
  October 31, at a half after seven."

But as Maida ceased gradually to worry about Laura, she began to be troubled about Rosie. For Rosie was not the same child. Much of the time she was silent, moody and listless.

One afternoon she came over to the shop, bringing the Clark twins with her. For awhile she and Maida played "house" with the little girls. Suddenly, Rosie tired of this game and sent the children home. Then for a time, she frolicked with Fluff while Maida read aloud. As suddenly as she had stopped playing "house" she interrupted Maida.

"Don't read any more," she commanded, "I want to talk with you."

Maida had felt the whole afternoon that there was something on Rosie's mind for whenever the scowl came between Rosie's eyebrows, it meant trouble. Maida closed her book and sat waiting.

"Maida," Rosie asked, "do you remember your mother?"

"Oh, yes," Maida answered, "perfectly. She was very beautiful. I could not forget her any more than a wonderful picture. She used to come and kiss me every night before she went to dinner with papa. She always smelled so sweet--whenever I see any flowers, I think of her. And she wore such beautiful dresses and jewels. She loved sparkly things, I guess--sometimes she looked like a fairy queen. Once she had a new lace gown all made of roses of lace and she had a diamond fastened in every rose to make it look like dew. When her hair was down, it came to her knees. She let me brush it sometimes with her gold brush."

"A gold brush," Rosie said in an awed tone.

"Yes, it was gold with her initials in diamonds on it. Papa gave her a whole set one birthday."

"How old were you when she died?" Rosie asked after a pause in which her scowl grew deeper.

"Eight."

"What did she die of?"

"I don't know," Maida answered. "You see I was so little that I didn't understand about dying. I had never heard of it. They told me one day that my mother had gone away. I used to ask every day when she was coming back and they'd say 'next week' and 'next week' and 'next week' until one day I got so impatient that I cried. Then they told me that my mother was living far away in a beautiful country and she would never come back. They said that I must not cry for she still loved me and was always watching over me. It was a great comfort to know that and of course I never cried after that for fear of worrying her. But at first it was very lonely. Why, Rosie--" She stopped terrified. "What's the matter?"

Rosie had thrown herself on the couch, and was crying bitterly. "Oh, Maida," she sobbed, "that's exactly what they say to me when I ask them--'next week' and 'next week' and 'next week' until I'm sick of it. My mother is dead and I know it."

"Oh, Rosie!" Maida protested. "Oh no, no, no--your mother is not dead. I can't believe it. I won't believe it."

"She is," Rosie persisted. "I know she is. Oh, what shall I do? Think how naughty I was! What shall I do?" She sobbed so convulsively that Maida was frightened.

"Listen, Rosie," she said. "You don't *know* your mother is dead. And I for one don't believe that she is."

"But they said the same thing to you," Rosie protested passionately.

"I think it was because I was sick," Maida said after a moment in which she thought the matter out. "They were afraid that I might die if they told me the truth. But whether your mother is alive or dead, the only way you can make up for being naughty is to be as good to your Aunt Theresa as you can. Oh, Rosie, please go to school every day."

"Do you suppose I could ever hook jack again?" Rosie asked bitterly. She dried her eyes. "I guess I'll go home now," she said, "and see if I can help Aunt Theresa with the supper. And I'm going to get her to teach me how to cook everything so that I can help mother--if she ever comes home."

The next day Rosie came into the shop with the happiest look that she had worn for a long time.

"I peeled the potatoes for Aunt Theresa, last night," she announced, "and set the table and wiped the dishes. She was real surprised. She asked me what had got into me?"

"I'm glad," Maida approved.

"I asked her when mother was coming back and she said the same thing, 'Next week, I think.'" Rosie's lip quivered.

"I think she'll come back, Rosie," Maida insisted. "And now let's not talk any more about it. Let's come out to play."

Mindful of her own lecture on obedience to Rosie, Maida skipped home the first time Granny rang the bell.

Granny met her at the door. Her eyes were shining with mischief. "You've got a visitor," she said. Maida could see that she was trying to keep her lips prim at the corners. She wondered who it was. Could it be--

She ran into the living-room. Her father jumped up from the easy-chair to meet her.

"Well, well, well, Miss Rosy-Cheeks. No need to ask how you are!" he said kissing her.

"Oh papa, papa, I never was so happy in all my life. If you could only be here with me all the time, there wouldn't be another thing in the world that I wanted. Don't you think you could give up Wall Street and come to live in this Court? You might open a shop too. Papa, I know you'd make a good shop-keeper although it isn't so easy as a lot of people think. But I'd teach you all I know--and, then, it's such fun. You could have a big shop for I know just how you like big things--just as I like little ones."

"Buffalo" Westabrook laughed. "I may have to come to it yet but it doesn't look like it this moment. My gracious, Posie, how you have improved! I never would know you for the same child. Where did you get those dimples? I never saw them in your face before. Your mother had them, though."

The shadow, that the mention of her mother's name always brought, darkened his face. "How you are growing to look like her!" he said.

Maida knew that she must not let him stay sad. "Dimples!" she squealed. "Really, papa?" She ran over to the mirror, climbed up on a chair and peeked in. Her face fell. "I don't see any," she said mournfully.

"And you're losing your limp," Mr. Westabrook said. Then catching sight of her woe-begone face, he laughed. "That's because you've stopped smiling, you little goose," he said. "Grin and you'll see them."

Obedient, Maida grinned so hard that it hurt. But the grin softened to a smile of perfect happiness. For, sure enough, pricking through the round of her soft, pink cheeks, were a pair of tiny hollows.

CHAPTER XI: HALLOWEEN

Halloween fell on Saturday that year. That made Friday a very busy time for Maida and the other members of the W.M.N.T. In the afternoon, they all worked like beavers making jack-o'-lanterns of the dozen pumpkins that Granny had ordered. Maida and Rosie and Dicky hollowed and scraped them. Arthur did all the hard work--the cutting out of the features, the putting-in of candle-holders. These pumpkin lanterns were for decoration. But Maida had ordered many paper jack-o'-lanterns for sale. The W.M.N.T.'s spent the evening rearranging the shop. Maida went to bed so tired that she could hardly drag one foot after the other. Granny had to undress her.

But when the school-children came flocking in the next morning, she felt more than repaid for her work. The shop resounded with the "Oh mys," and "Oh looks," of their surprise and delight.

Indeed, the room seemed full of twinkling yellow faces. Lines of them grinned in the doorway. Rows of them smirked from the shelves. A frieze, close-set as peas in a pod, grimaced from the molding. The jolly-looking pumpkin jacks, that Arthur had made, were piled in a pyramid in the window. The biggest of them all--"he looks just like the man in the moon," Rosie said--smiled benignantly at the passers-by from the top of the heap. Standing about everywhere among the lanterns were groups of little paper brownies, their tiny heads turned upwards as if, in the greatest astonishment, they were examining these monster beings.

The jack-o'-lanterns sold like hot cakes. As for the brownies, "Granny, you'd think they were marching off the shelves!" Maida said. By dark, she was diving breathlessly into her surplus stock. At the first touch of twilight, she lighted every lantern left in the place. Five minutes afterwards, a crowd of children had gathered to gaze at the flaming faces in the window. Even the grown-ups stopped to admire the effect.

More customers came and more--a great many children whom Maida had never seen before. By six o'clock, she had sold out her entire stock. When she sat down to dinner that night, she was a very happy little girl.

"This is the best day I've had since I opened the shop," she said contentedly. She was not tired, though. "I feel just like going to a party to-night. Granny, can I wear my prettiest Roman sash?"

"You can wear annyt'ing you want, my lamb," Granny said, "for 'tis the good, busy little choild you've been this day."

Granny dressed her according to Maida's choice, in white. A very, simple, soft little frock, it was, with many tiny tucks made by hand and many insertions of a beautiful, fine lace. Maida chose to wear with it pale blue silk stockings and slippers, a sash of blue, striped in pink and white, a string of pink Venetian beads.

"Now, Granny, I'll read until the children call for me," she suggested, "so I won't rumple my dress."

But she was too excited to read. She sat for a long time at the window, just looking out. Presently the jack-o'-lanterns, lighted now, began to make blobs of gold in the furry darkness of the street. She could not at first make out who held them. It was strange to watch the fiery, grinning heads, flying, bodiless, from place to place. But she identified the lanterns in the court by the houses from which they emerged. The three small ones on the end at the left meant Dicky and Molly and Tim. Two big ones, mounted on sticks, came from across the way--Rosie and Arthur, of course. Two, just alike, trotting side by side betrayed the Clark twins. A baby-lantern, swinging close to the ground--that could be nobody but Betsy.

The crowd in the Court began to march towards the shop. For an instant, Maida watched the spots of brilliant color dancing in her direction. Then she slipped into her coat, and seized her own lantern. When she came outside, the sidewalk seemed crowded with grotesque faces, all laughing at her.

"Just think," she said, "I have never been to a Halloween party in my life."

"You are the queerest thing, Maida," Rosie said in perplexity. "You've been to Europe. You can talk French and Italian. And yet, you've never been to a Halloween party. Did you ever hang May-baskets?"

Maida shook her head.

"You wait until next May," Rosie prophesied gleefully.

The crowd crossed over into the Court Two motionless, yellow faces, grinning at them from the Lathrop steps, showed that Laura and Harold had come out to meet them. On the lawn they broke into an impromptu game of tag which the jack-o'-lanterns seemed to enjoy as much as the children: certainly, they whizzed from place to place as quickly and, certainly, they smiled as hard.

The game ended, they left their lanterns on the piazza and trooped into the house.

"We've got to play the first games in the kitchen," Laura announced after the coats and hats had come off and Mrs. Lathrop had greeted them all.

Maida wondered what sort of party it was that was held in the kitchen but she asked no questions. Almost bursting with curiosity, she joined the long line marching to the back of the house.

In the middle of the kitchen floor stood a tub of water with apples floating in it.

"Bobbing for apples!" the children exclaimed. "Oh, that's the greatest fun of all. Did you ever bob for apples, Maida?"

"No."

"Let Maida try it first, then," Laura said. "It's very easy, Maida," she went on with twinkling eyes. "All you have to do is to kneel on the floor, clasp your hands behind you, and pick out one of the apples with your teeth. You'll each be allowed three minutes."

"Oh, I can get a half a dozen in three minutes, I guess," Maida said.

Laura tied a big apron around Maida's waist and stood, watch in hand. The children gathered in a circle about the tub. Maida knelt on the floor, clasped her hands behind her and reached with a wide-open mouth for the nearest apple. But at the first touch of her lips, the apple bobbed away. She reached for another. That bobbed away, too. Another and another and another--they all bobbed clean out of her reach, no matter how delicately she touched them. That method was unsuccessful.

"One minute," called Laura.

Maida could hear the children giggling at her. She tried another scheme, making vicious little dabs at the apples. Her beads and her hair-ribbon and one of her long curls dipped into the water. But she only succeeded in sending the apples spinning across the tub.

"Two minutes!" called Laura.

"Why don't you get those half a dozen," the children jeered. "You know you said it was so easy."

Maida giggled too. But inwardly, she made up her mind that she would get one of those apples if she dipped her whole head into the tub. At last a brilliant idea occurred to her. Using her chin as a guide, she poked a big rosy apple over against the side of the tub. Wedging it there against another big apple, she held it tight. Then she dropped her head a little, gave a sudden big bite and arose amidst applause, with the apple secure between her teeth.

After that she had the fun of watching the other children. The older ones were adepts. In three minutes, Rosie secured four, Dicky five and Arthur six. Rosie did not get a drop of water on her but the boys emerged with dripping heads. The little children were not very successful but they were more fun. Molly swallowed so much water that she choked and had to be patted on the back. Betsy after a few snaps of her little, rosebud mouth, seized one of the apples with her hand, sat down on the floor and calmly ate it. But the climax was reached when Tim Doyle suddenly lurched forward and fell headlong into the tub.

"I knew he'd fall in," Molly said in a matter-of-fact voice. "He always falls into everything. I brought a dry set of clothes for him. Come, Tim!"

At this announcement, everybody shrieked. Molly disappeared with Tim in the direction of Laura's bedroom. When she reappeared, sure enough, Tim had a dry suit on.

Next Laura ordered them to sit about the kitchen-table. She gave each child an apple and a knife and directed him to pare the apple without breaking the peel. If you think that is an easy thing to do, try it. It seemed to Maida that she never would accomplish it. She spoiled three apples before she succeeded.

"Now take your apple-paring and form in line across the kitchen-floor," Laura commanded.

The flock scampered to obey her.

"Now when I say 'Three!'" she continued, "throw the parings back over your shoulder to the floor. If the paring makes a letter, it will be the initial of your future husband or wife. One! *Two*! THREE!"

A dozen apple-parings flew to the floor. Everybody raced across the room to examine the results.

"Mine is B," Dicky said.

"And mine's an O," Rosie declared, "as plain as anything. What's yours, Maida?"

"It's an X," Maida answered in great perplexity. "I don't believe that there are any names beginning with X except Xenophon and Xerxes."

"Well, mine's as bad," Laura laughed, "it's a Z. I guess I'll be Mrs. Zero."

"That's nothing," Arthur laughed, "mine's an &--I can't marry anybody named ----'and.'"

"Well, if that isn't successful," Laura said, "there's another way of finding out who your husband or wife's going to be. You must walk down the cellar-stairs backwards with a candle in one hand and a mirror in the other. You must look in the mirror all the time and, when you get to the foot of the stairs, you will see, reflected in it, the face of your husband or wife."

This did not interest the little children but the big ones were wild to try it.

"Gracious, doesn't it sound scary?" Rosie said, her great eyes snapping. "I love a game that's kind of spooky, don't you, Maida?"

Maida did not answer. She was watching Harold who was sneaking out of the room very quietly from a door at the side.

"All right, then, Rosie," Laura caught her up, "you can go first."

The children all crowded over to the door leading to the cellar. The stairs were as dark as pitch. Rosie took the mirror and the candle that Laura handed her and slipped through the opening. The little audience listened breathless.

They heard Rosie stumble awkwardly down the stairs, heard her pause at the foot. Next came a moment of silence, of waiting as tense above as below. Then came a burst of Rosie's jolly laughter. She came running up to them, her cheeks like roses, her eyes like stars.

They crowded around her. "What did you see?" "Tell us about it?" they clamored.

Rosie shook her head. "No, no, no," she maintained, "I'm not going to tell you what I saw until you've been down yourself."

It was Arthur's turn next. They listened again. The same thing happened--awkward stumbling down the stairs, a pause, then a roar of laughter.

"Oh what did you see?" they implored when he reappeared.

"Try it yourself!" he advised. "I'm not going to tell."

Dicky went next. Again they all listened and to the same mysterious doings. Dicky came back smiling but, like the others, he refused to describe his experiences.

Now it was Maida's turn. She took the candle and the mirror from Dicky and plunged into the shivery darkness of the stairs. It was doubly difficult for her to go down backwards because of her lameness. But she finally arrived at the bottom and stood there expectantly. It seemed a long time before anything happened. Suddenly, she felt something stir back of her. A lighted jack-o'-lantern came from between the folds of a curtain which hung from the ceiling. It grinned over her shoulder at her face in the mirror.

Maida burst into a shriek of laughter and scrambled upstairs. "I'm going to marry a jack-o'-lantern," she said. "My name's going to be Mrs. Jack Pumpkin."

"I'm going to marry Laura's sailor-doll," Rosie confessed. "My name is Mrs. Yankee Doodle."

"I'm going to marry Laura's big doll, Queenie," Arthur admitted.

"And I'm going to marry Harold's Teddy-bear," Dicky said.

After that they blew soap-bubbles and roasted apples and chestnuts, popped corn and pulled candy at the great fireplace in the playroom. And at Maida's request, just before they left, Laura danced for them.

"Will you help me to get on my costume, Maida?" Laura asked.

"Of course," Maida said, wondering.

"I asked you to come down here, Maida," Laura said when the two little girls were alone, "because I wanted to tell you that I am sorry for the way I treated you just before I got diphtheria. I told my mother about it and she said I did those things because I was coming down sick. She said that people are always fretty and cross when they're not well. But I don't think it was all that. I guess I did it on purpose just to be disagreeable. But I hope you will excuse me."

"Of course I will, Laura," Maida said heartily. "And I hope you will forgive me for going so long without speaking to you. But you see I heard," she stopped and hesitated, "things," she ended lamely.

"Oh, I know what you heard. I said those things about you to the W.M.N.T.'s so that they'd get back to you. I wanted to hurt your feelings." Laura in her turn stopped and hesitated for an instant. "I was jealous," she finally confessed in a burst. "But I want you to understand this, Maida. I didn't believe those horrid things myself. I always have a feeling inside when people are telling lies and I didn't have that feeling when you were talking to me. I knew you were telling the truth. And all the time while I was getting well, I felt so dreadfully about it that I knew I never would be happy again unless I told you so."

"I did feel bad when I heard those things," Maida said, "but of course I forgot about them when Rosie told me you were ill. Let's forget all about it again."

But Maida told the W.M.N.T.'s something of her talk with Laura and the result was an invitation to Laura to join the club. It was accepted gratefully.

The next month went by on wings. It was a busy month although in a way, it was an uneventful one. The weather kept clear and fine. Little rain fell but, on the other hand, to the great disappointment of the little people of Primrose Court, there was no snow. Maida saw nothing of her father for business troubles kept him in New York. He wrote constantly to her and she wrote as faithfully to him. Letters could not quite fill the gap that his absence made. Perhaps Billy suspected Maida's secret loneliness for he came oftener and oftener to see her.

One night the W.M.N.T.'s begged so hard for a story that he finally began one called "The Crystal Ball." A wonderful thing about it was that it was half-game and half-story. Most wonderful of all, it went on from night to night and never showed any signs of coming to an end. But in order to play this game-story, there were two or three conditions to which you absolutely must submit. For instance, it must always be played in the dark. And first, everybody must shut his eyes tight. Billy would say in a deep voice, "Abracadabra!" and, presto, there they all were, Maida, Rosie, Laura, Billy, Arthur and Dicky inside the crystal ball. What people lived there and what things happened to them can not be told here. But after an hour or more, Billy's deepest voice would boom, "Abracadabra!" again and, presto, there they all were again, back in the cheerful living-room.

Maida hoped against hope that her father would come to spend Thanksgiving with her but that, he wrote finally, was impossible. Billy came, however, and they three enjoyed one of Granny's delicious turkey dinners.

"I hoped that I would have found your daughter Annie by this time, Granny," Billy said. "I ask every Irishman I meet if he came from Aldigarey, County Sligo or if he knows anybody who did, or if he's ever met a pretty Irish girl by the name of Annie Flynn. But I'll find her yet--you'll see."

"I hope so, Misther Billy," Granny said respectfully. But Maida thought her voice sounded as if she had no great hope.

Dicky still continued to come for his reading-lessons, although Maida could see that, in a month or two, he would not need a teacher. The quiet, studious, pale little boy had become a great favorite with Granny Flynn.

"Sure an' Oi must be after getting over to see the poor lad's mother some noi-ght," she said. "'Tis a noice woman she must be wid such a pretty-behaved little lad."

"Oh, she is, Granny," Maida said earnestly. "I've been there once or twice when Mrs. Dore came home early. And she's just the nicest lady and so fond of Dicky and the baby."

But Granny was old and very easily tired and, so, though her intentions were of the best, she did not make this call.

One afternoon, after Thanksgiving, Maida ran over to Dicky's to borrow some pink tissue paper. She knocked gently. Nobody answered. But from the room came the sound of sobbing. Maida listened. It was Dicky's voice. At first she did not know what to do. Finally, she opened the door and peeped in. Dicky was sitting all crumpled up, his head resting on the table.

"Oh, what is the matter, Dicky?" Maida asked.

Dicky jumped. He raised his head and looked at her. His face was swollen with crying, his eyes red and heavy. For a moment he could not speak. Maida could see that he was ashamed of being caught in tears, that he was trying hard to control himself.

"It's something I heard," he replied at last.

"What?" Maida asked.

"Last night after I got to bed, Doc O'Brien came here to get his bill paid. Mother thought I was asleep and asked him a whole lot of questions. He told her that I wasn't any better and I never would be any better. He said that I'd be a cripple for the rest of my life."

In spite of all his efforts, Dicky's voice broke into a sob.

"Oh Dicky, Dicky," Maida said. Better than anybody else in the world, Maida felt that she could understand, could sympathize. "Oh, Dicky, how sorry I am!"

"I can't bear it," Dicky said.

He put his head down on the table and began to sob. "I can't bear it," he said. "Why, I thought when I grew up to be a man, I was going to take care of mother and Delia. Instead of that, they'll be taking care of me. What can a cripple do? Once I read about a crippled newsboy. Do you suppose I could sell papers?" he asked with a gleam of hope.

"I'm sure you could," Maida said heartily, "and a great many other things. But it may not be as bad as you think, Dicky. Dr. O'Brien may be mistaken. You know something was wrong with me when I was born and I did not begin to walk until a year ago. My father has taken me to so many doctors that I'm sure he could not remember half their names. But they all said the same thing--that I never would walk like other children. Then a very great physician--Dr. Greinschmidt--came from away across the sea, from Germany. He said he could cure me and he did. I had to be operated on and--oh--I suffered dreadfully. But you see that I'm all well now. I'm even losing my limp. Now, I believe that Doctor Greinschmidt can cure you. The next time my father comes home I'm going to ask him."

Dicky had stopped crying. He was drinking down everything that she said. "Is he still here--that doctor?" he asked.

"No," Maida admitted sorrowfully. "But there must be doctors as good as he somewhere. But don't you worry about it at all, Dicky. You wait until my father sees you--he always gets everything made right."

"When's your father coming home?"

"I don't quite know--but I look for him any time now."

Dicky started to set the table. "I guess I wouldn't have cried," he said after a while, "if I could have cried last night when I first heard it. But of course I couldn't let mother or Doc O'Brien know that I'd heard them--it would make them feel bad. I don't want my mother ever to know that I know it."

After that, Maida redoubled her efforts to be nice to Dicky. She cudgeled her brains too for new decorative schemes for his paper-work. She asked Billy Potter to bring a whole bag of her books from the Beacon Street house and she lent them to Dicky, a half dozen at a time.

Indeed, they were a very busy quartette--the W.M.N.T.'s. Rosie went to school every day. She climbed out of her window no more at night. She seemed to prefer helping Maida in the shop to anything else. Arthur Duncan was equally industrious. With no Rosie to play hookey with, he, too, was driven to attending school regularly. His leisure hours were devoted to his whittling and wood-carving. He was always doing kind things for Maida and Granny, bringing up the coal, emptying the ashes, running errands.

And so November passed into December.

CHAPTER XII: THE FIRST SNOW

L ook out the window, my lamb," Granny called one morning early in December. Maida opened her eyes, jumped obediently out of bed and pattered across the room. There, she gave a scream of delight, jumping up and down and clapping her hands.

"Snow! Oh goody, goody, goody! Snow at last!"

It looked as if the whole world had been wrapped in a blanket of the whitest, fleeciest, shiningest wool. Sidewalks, streets, crossings were all leveled to one smoothness. The fences were so muffled that they had swelled to twice their size. The houses wore trim, pointy caps on their gables. The high bushes in the yard hung to the very ground. The low ones had become mounds. The trees looked as if they had been packed in cotton-wool and put away for the winter.

"And the lovely part of it is, it's still snowing," Maida exclaimed blissfully.

"Glory be, it'ull be a blizzard before we're t'rough wid ut," Granny said and shivered.

Maida dressed in the greatest excitement. Few children came in to make purchases that morning and the lines pouring into the schoolhouse were very shivery and much shorter than usual. At a quarter to twelve, the one-session bell rang. When the children came out of school at one, the snow was whirling down thicker and faster than in the morning. A high wind came up and piled it in the most unexpected places. Trade stopped entirely in the shop. No mother would let her children brave so terrific a storm.

It snowed that night and all the next morning. The second day fewer children went to school than on the first. But at two o'clock when the sun burst through the gray sky, the children swarmed the streets. Shovels and brooms began to appear, snow-balls to fly, sleigh-bells to tinkle.

Rosie came dashing into the shop in the midst of this burst of excitement. "I've shoveled our sidewalk," she announced triumphantly. "Is anything wrong with me? Everybody's staring at me."

Maida stared too. Rosie's scarlet cape was dotted with snow, her scarlet hat was white with it. Great flakes had caught in her long black hair, had starred her soft brows--they hung from her very eyelashes. Her cheeks and lips were the color of coral and her eyes like great velvety moons.

"You look in the glass and see what they're staring at," Maida said slyly. Rosie went to the mirror.

"I don't see anything the matter."

"It's because you look so pretty, goose!" Maida exclaimed.

Rosie always blushed and looked ashamed if anybody alluded to her prettiness. Now she leaped to Maida's side and pretended to beat her.

"Stop that!" a voice called. Startled, the little girls looked up. Billy stood in the doorway. "I've come over to make a snow-house," he explained.

"Oh, Billy, what things you do think of!" Maida exclaimed. "Wait till I get Arthur and Dicky!"

"Couldn't get many more in here, could we?" Billy commented when the five had assembled in the "child's size" yard. "I don't know that we could stow away another shovel. Now, first of all, you're to pile all the snow in the yard into that corner."

Everybody went to work. But Billy and Arthur moved so quickly with their big shovels that Maida and Rosie and Dicky did nothing but hop about them. Almost before they realized it, the snow-pile reached to the top of the fence.

"Pack it down hard," Billy commanded, "as hard as you can make it."

Everybody scrambled to obey. For a few moments the sound of shovels beating on the snow drowned their talk.

"That will do for that," Billy commanded suddenly. His little force stopped, breathless and red-cheeked. "Now I'm going to dig out the room. I guess I'll have to do this. If you're not careful enough, the roof will cave in. Then it's all got to be done again."

Working very slowly, he began to hollow out the structure. After the hole had grown big enough, he crawled into it. But in spite of his own warning, he must have been too energetic in his movements. Suddenly the roof came down on his head.

Billy was on his feet in an instant, shaking the snow off as a dog shakes off water.

"Why, Billy, you look like a snow-man," Maida laughed.

"I feel like one," Billy said, wiping the snow from his eyes and from under his collar. "But don't be discouraged, my hearties, up with it again. I'll be more careful the next time."

They went at it again with increased interest, heaping up a mound of snow bigger than before, beating it until it was as hard as a brick, hollowing out inside a chamber big enough for three of them to occupy at once. But Billy gave them no time to enjoy their new dwelling.

"Run into the house," was his next order, "and bring out all the water you can carry."

There was a wild scramble to see which would get to the sink first but in a few moments, an orderly file emerged from the house, Arthur with a bucket, Dicky with a basin, Rosie with the dish-pan, Maida with a dipper.

"Now I'm going to pour water over the house," Billy explained. "You see if it freezes now it will last longer." Very carefully, he sprayed it on the sides and roof, dashing it upwards on the inside walls:

"We might as well make it look pretty while we're about it," Billy continued. "You children get to work and make a lot of snow-balls the size of an orange and just as round as you can turn them out."

This was easy work. Before Billy could say, "Jack Robinson!" four pairs of eager hands had accumulated snow-balls enough for a sham battle. In the meantime, Billy had decorated the doorway with two tall, round pillars. He added a pointed roof to the house and trimmed it with snow-balls, all along the edge.

"Now I guess we'd better have a snow-man to live in this mansion while we're about it," Billy suggested briskly. "Each of you roll up an arm or a leg while I make the body."

Billy placed the legs in the corner opposite the snow-house. He lifted on to them the big round body which he himself had rolled. Putting the arms on was not so easy. He worked for a long time before he found the angle at which they would stick.

Everybody took a hand at the head. Maida contributed some dulse for the hair, slitting it into ribbons, which she stuck on with glue. Rosie found a broken clothes-pin for the nose. The round, smooth coals that Dicky discovered in the coal-hod made a pair of expressive black eyes. Arthur cut two sets of teeth from orange peel and inserted them in the gash that was the mouth. When the head was set on the shoulders, Billy disappeared into the house for a moment. He came back carrying a suit-case. "Shut your eyes, every manjack of you," he ordered. "You're not to see what I do until it's done. If I catch one of you peeking, I'll confine you in the snow-house for five minutes."

The W.M.N.T.'s shut their eyes tight and held down the lids with resolute fingers. But they kept their ears wide open. The mysterious work on which Billy was engaged was accompanied by the most tantalizing noises.

"Oh, Billy, can't I please look," Maida begged, jiggling up and down. "I can't stand it much longer."

"In a minute," Billy said encouragingly. The mysterious noises kept up. "Now," Billy said suddenly.

Four pairs of eyes leaped open. Four pairs of lips shrieked their delight. Indeed, Maida and Rosie laughed so hard that they finally rolled in the snow.

Billy had put an old coat on the snow-man's body. He had put a tall hat-- Arthur called it a "stove-pipe"--on the snow-man's head. He had put an old black pipe between the snow-man's grinning, orange-colored teeth. Gloves hung limply from the snow-man's arm-stumps and to one of them a cane was fastened. Billy had managed to give the snow-man's head a cock to one side. Altogether he looked so spruce and jovial that it was impossible not to like him.

"Mr. Chumpleigh, ladies and gentlemen," Billy said. "Some members of the W.M.N.T., Mr. Chumpleigh."

And Mr. Chumpleigh, he was until--until--

Billy stayed that night to dinner. They had just finished eating when an excited ring of the bell announced Rosie.

"Oh, Granny," she said, "the boys have made a most wonderful coast down Halliwell Street and Aunt Theresa says I can go coasting until nine o'clock if you'll let Maida go too. I thought maybe you would, especially if Billy comes along."

"If Misther Billy goes, 'twill be all roight."

"Oh, Granny," Maida said, "you dear, darling, old fairy-dame!" She was so excited that she wriggled like a little eel all the time Granny was bundling her into her clothes. And when she reached the street, it seemed as if she must explode.

A big moon, floating like a silver balloon in the sky, made the night like day. The neighborhood sizzled with excitement for the street and sidewalks were covered with children dragging sleds.

"It's like the 'Pied Piper', Rosie," Maida said joyfully, "children everywhere and all going in the same direction."

They followed the procession up Warrington Street to where Halliwell Street sloped down the hill.

Billy let out a long whistle of astonishment. "Great Scott, what a coast!" he said.

In the middle of the street was a ribbon of ice three feet wide and as smooth as glass. At the foot of the hill, a piled-up mound of snow served as a buffer.

"The boys have been working on the slide all day," Rosie said. "Did you ever see such a nice one, Maida?"

"I never saw any kind of a one," Maida confessed. "How did they make it so smooth?"

"Pouring water on it."

"Have you never coasted before, Maida?" Billy asked.

"Never."

"Well, here's your chance then," said a cheerful voice back of them. They all turned. There stood Arthur Duncan with what Maida soon learned was a "double-runner."

Billy examined it carefully. "Did you make it, Arthur?"

"Yes."

"Pretty good piece of work," Billy commented. "Want to try it, Maida?"

"I'm crazy to!"

"All right. Pile on!"

Arthur took his place in front. Rosie sat next, then Dicky, then Maida, then Billy.

"Hold on to Dicky," Billy instructed Maida, "and I'll hold on to you."

Tingling with excitement, Maida did as she was told. But it seemed as if they would never start. But at last, she heard Billy's voice, "On your marks. Get set! Go!" The double-runner stirred.

It moved slowly for a moment across the level top of the street. Then came the first slope of the hill--they plunged forward. She heard Rosie's hysterical shriek, Dicky's vociferous cheers and Billy's blood-curdling yells, but she herself was as silent as a little image. They struck the second slope of the hill--then she screamed, too. The houses on either side shot past like pictures in the kinetoscope. She felt a rush of wind that must surely blow her ears off. They reached the third slope of the hill--and now they had left the earth and were sailing through the air. The next instant the double-runner had come to rest on the bank of snow and Rosie and she were hugging each other and saying, "Wasn't it GREAT?"

They climbed to the top of the hill again. All the way back, Maida watched the sleds whizzing down the coast, boys alone on sleds, girls alone on sleds, pairs of girls, pairs of boys, one seated in front, the other steering with a foot that trailed be-hind on the ice, timid little girls who did not dare the ice but contented themselves with sliding on the snow at either side, daring little boys who went down lying flat on their sleds.

At the top they were besieged with entreaties to go on the double-runner and, as there was room enough for one more, they took a little boy or girl with them each time. Rosie lent her sled to those who had none. At first there were plenty of these, standing at the top of the coast, wistfully watching the fun of more fortunate children. But after a while it was discovered that the ice was so smooth that almost anything could be used for coasting. The sledless ones rushed home and reappeared with all kinds of things. One little lad went down on a shovel and his intrepid little sister followed on a broom. Boxes and shingles and even dish-pans began to appear. Most reckless of all, one big fellow slid down on his two feet, landing in a heap in the snow.

Maida enjoyed every moment of it--even the long walks back up the hill. Once the double-runner struck into a riderless sled that had drifted on to the course, and was overturned immediately. Nobody was hurt. Rosie, Dicky and Arthur were cast safely to one side in the soft snow. But Maida and Billy were thrown, whirling, on to the ice. Billy kept his grip on Maida and they shot down the hill, turning round and round and round. At first Maida was a little frightened. But when she saw that they were perfectly safe, that Billy was making her spin about in that ridiculous fashion, she laughed so hard that she was weak when they reached the bottom.

"Oh, do let's do that again!" she said when she caught her breath.

Never was such a week as followed. The cold weather kept up. Continued storms added to the snow. For the first time in years came four one-session days in a single week. It seemed as if Jack Frost were on the side of the children. He would send violent flurries of snow just before the one-session bell rang but as soon as the children were safely on the street, the sun would come out bright as summer.

Every morning when Maida woke up, she would say to herself, "I wonder how Mr. Chumpleigh is to-day." Then she would run over to the window to see.

Mr. Chumpleigh had become a great favorite in the neighborhood. He was so tall that his round, happy face with its eternal orange-peel grin could look straight over the fence to the street. The passers-by used to stop, paralyzed by the vision. But after studying the phenomenon, they would go laughing on their way. Occasionally a bad boy would shy a snow-ball at the smiling countenance but Mr. Chumpleigh was so hard-headed that nothing seemed to hurt him. In the course of time, the "stove-pipe" became very battered and, as the result of continued storms, one eye sank down to the middle of his cheek. But in spite of these injuries, he continued to maintain his genial grin.

"Let's go out and fix Mr. Chumpleigh," Rosie would say every day. The two little girls would brush the snow off his hat and coat, adjust his nose and teeth, would straighten him up generally.

After a while, Maida threw her bird-crumbs all over Mr. Chumpleigh. Thereafter, the saucy little English sparrows ate from Mr. Chumpleigh's hat-brim, his pipe-bowl, even his pockets.

"Perhaps the snow will last all winter," Maida said hopefully one day. "If it does, Mr. Chumpleigh's health will be perfect."

"Well, perhaps, it's just as well if he goes," Rosie said sensibly; "we haven't done a bit of work since he came."

On Sunday the weather moderated a little. Mr. Chumpleigh bore a most melancholy look all the afternoon as if he feared what was to come. What was worse, he lost his nose.

Monday morning, Maida ran to the window dreading what she might see. But instead of the thaw she expected, a most beautiful sight spread out before her. The weather had turned cold in the night. Everything that had started to melt had frozen up again. The sidewalks were liked frosted cakes. Long icicles made pretty fringes around the roofs of the houses. The trees and bushes were glazed by a sheathing of crystal. The sunlight playing through all this turned the world into a heap of diamonds.

Mr. Chumpleigh had perked up under the influence of the cold. His manner had gained in solidity although his gaze was a little glassy. Hopefully Maida hunted about until she found his nose.

She replaced his old set with some new orange-peel teeth and stuck his pipe between them. He looked quite himself.

But, alas, the sun came out and melted the whole world. The sidewalks trickled streams. The icicles dripped away in showers of diamonds. The trees lost their crystal sheathing.

In the afternoon, Mr. Chumpleigh began to droop. By night his head was resting disconsolately on his own shoulder. When Maida looked out the next morning, there was nothing in the corner but a mound of snow. An old coat lay to one side. Strewn about were a hat, a pair of gloves, a pipe and a cane.

Mr. Chumpleigh had passed away in the night.

CHAPTER XIII: THE FAIR

SAVE YOUR PENNIES
A CHRISTMAS FAIR
WILL BE HELD IN THIS SHOP
THE SATURDAY BEFORE
CHRISTMAS
DELICIOUS CANDIES MADE BY
MISS ROSIE BRINE
PAPER GOODS DESIGNED AND
EXECUTED BY
MASTER RICHARD DORE
WOOD CARVING DESIGNED AND
EXECUTED BY
MASTER ARTHUR DUNCAN
DON'T MISS IT!

This sign hung in Maida's window for a week. Billy made it. The lettering was red and gold. In one corner, he painted a picture of a little boy and girl in their nightgowns peeking up a chimney-place hung with stockings. In the other corner, the full-moon face of a Santa Claus popped like a jolly jack-in-the-box from a chimney-top. A troop of reindeer, dragging a sleigh full of toys, scurried through the printing. The whole thing was enclosed in a wreath of holly.

The sign attracted a great deal of attention. Children were always stopping to admire it and even grown-people paused now and then. There was such a falling-off of Maida's trade that she guessed that the children were really saving their pennies for the fair. This delighted her.

The W.M.N.T.'s wasted no time that last week in spite of a very enticing snow-storm. Maida, of course, had nothing to do on her own account, but she worked with Dicky, morning and afternoon.

Rosie could not make candy until the last two or three days for fear it would get stale. Then she set to like a little whirlwind.

"My face is almost tanned from bending over the stove," she said to Maida; "Aunt Theresa says if I cook another batch of candy, I'll have a crop of freckles."

Arthur seemed to work the hardest of all because his work was so much more difficult. It took a great deal of time and strength and yet nobody could help him in it. The sound of his hammering came into Maida's room early in the morning. It came in sometimes late at night when, cuddling between her blankets, she thought what a happy girl she was.

"I niver saw such foine, busy little folks," Granny said approvingly again and again. "It moinds me av me own Annie. Niver a moment but that lass was working at some t'ing. Oh, I wonder what she's doun' and finking this Christmas."

"Don't you worry," Maida always said. "Billy'll find her for you yet--he said he would."

Maida, herself, was giving, for the first time in her experience, a good deal of thought to Christmas time.

In the first place, she had sent the following invitation to every child in Prim-rose Court:

"Will you please come to my Christmas Tree to be given Christmas Night in the 'Little Shop.'   Maida."

In the second place, she was spying on all her friends, listening to their talk, watching them closely in work and play to find just the right thing to give them.

"Do you know, I never made a Christmas present in my life," she said one day to Rosie.

"You never made a Christmas present?" Rosie repeated.

Maida's quick perception sensed in Rosie's face an unspoken accusation of self-ishness.

"It wasn't because I didn't want to, Rosie dear," Maida hastened to explain. "It was because I was too sick. You see, I was always in bed. I was too weak to make anything and I could not go out and buy presents as other children did. But people used to give me the loveliest things."

"What did they give you?" Rosie asked curiously.

"Oh, all kinds of things. Father's given me an automobile and a pair of Shetland ponies and a family of twenty dolls and my weight in silver dollars. I can't remember half the things I've had."

"A pair of Shetland ponies, an automobile, a family of twenty dolls, your weight in silver dollars," Rosie repeated after her. "Why, Maida, you're dreaming or you're out of your head."

"Out of my head! Why, Rosie you're out of *your* head. Don't you suppose I know what I got for Christmas?" Maida's eyes began to flash and her lips to tremble.

"Well, now, Maida, just think of it," Rosie said in her most reasonable voice. "Here you are a little girl just like anybody else only you're running a shop. Now just as if you could afford to have an automobile! Why, my father knows a man who knows another man who bought an automobile and it cost nine hundred dollars. What did yours cost?"

"Two thousand dollars." Maida said this with a guilty air in spite of her knowledge of her own truth.

Rosie smiled roguishly. "Maida, dear," she coaxed, "you dreamed it."

Maida started to her feet. For a moment she came near saying something very saucy indeed. But she remembered in time. Of course nobody in the neighborhood knew that she was "Buffalo" Westabrook's daughter. It was impossible for her to prove any of her statements. The flash died out of her eyes. But another flash came into her cheeks--the flash of dimples.

"Well, perhaps I *did* dream it, Rosie," she said archly. "But I don't think I did," she added in a quiet voice.

Rosie turned the subject tactfully. "What are you going to give your father?" she asked.

"That's bothering me dreadfully," Maida sighed; "I can't think of anything he needs."

"Why don't you buy him the same thing I'm going to get my papa," Rosie suggested eagerly. "That is, I'm going to buy it if I make enough money at the fair. Does your father shave himself?"

"Oh, Adolph, his valet, always shaves him," Maida answered.

Rosie's brow knit over the word ***valet***--but Maida was always puzzling the neighborhood with strange expressions. Then her brow lightened. "My father goes to a barber, too," she said. "I've heard him complaining lots of times how expensive it is. And the other day Arthur told me about a razor his father uses. He says it's just like a lawn-mower or a carpet-sweeper. You don't have to have anybody shave you if you have one of them. You run it right over your face and it takes all the beard off and doesn't cut or anything. Now, wouldn't you think that would be fun?"

"I should think it would be just lovely," Maida agreed. "That's just the thing for papa--for he is so busy. How much does it cost, Rosie?"

"About a dollar, Arthur thought. I never paid so much for a Christmas present in my life. And I'm not sure yet that I can get one. But if I do sell two dollars worth of candy, I can buy something perfectly beautiful for both father and mother."

"Oh, Rosie," Maida asked breathlessly, "do you mean that your mother's come back?"

Rosie's face changed. "Don't you think I'd tell you that the first thing? No, she hasn't come back and they don't say anything about her coming back. But if she ever does come, I guess I'm going to have her Christmas present all ready for her."

Maida patted her hand. "She's coming back," she said; "I know it."

Rosie sighed. "You come down Main Street the night before Christmas. Dicky and I are going to buy our Christmas presents then and we can show you where to get the little razor."

"I'd love to." Maida beamed. And indeed, it seemed the most fascinating prospect in the world to her. Every night after she went to bed, she thought it over. She was really going to buy Christmas presents without any grown-up person about to interfere. It was rapture.

The night before the fair, the children worked even harder than the night before Halloween, for there were so many things to display. It was evident that the stock would overflow windows and shelves and show cases.

"We'll bring the long kitchen table in for your things, Arthur," Maida decided after a perplexed consideration of the subject. "Dicky's and Rosie's things ought to go on the shelves and into the show cases where nobody can handle them."

They tugged the table into the shop and covered it with a beautiful old blue counter-pane.

"That's fine!" Arthur approved, unpacking his handicraft from the bushel-baskets in which he brought them.

The others stood round admiring the treasures and helping him to arrange them prettily. A fleet of graceful little boats occupied one end of the table, piles of bread-boards, rolling-pins and "cats," the other. In the center lay a bowl filled with tiny baskets, carved from peach-stones. From the molding hung a fringe of hockey-sticks.

Having arranged all Arthur's things, the quartette filed upstairs to the closet where Dicky's paper-work was kept.

"Gracious, I didn't realize there were so many," Rosie said.

"Sure, the lad has worked day and night," Granny said, patting Dicky's thin cheek.

They filled Arthur's baskets and trooped back to the shop. They lined show case and shelves with the glittering things--boxes, big and little, gorgeously ornamented with stars and moons, caps of gold and silver, flying gay plumes, rainbow boats too beautiful to sail on anything but fairy seas, miniature jackets and trousers that only a circus rider would wear.

"Dicky, I never did see anything look so lovely," Maida said, shaking her hands with delight. "I really didn't realize how pretty they were."

Dicky's big eyes glowed with satisfaction. "Nor me neither," he confessed.

"And now," Maida said, bubbling over with suppressed importance, "Rosie's candies--I've saved that until the last." She pulled out one of the drawers under the show case and lifted it on to the counter. It was filled with candy-boxes of paper, prettily decorated with flower patterns on the outside, with fringes of lace paper on the inside. "I ordered these boxes for you, Rosie," she explained. "I knew your candy would sell better if it was put up nicely. I thought the little ones could be five-cent size, the middle-sized ones ten-cent size, and the big ones twenty-five cent size."

Rosie was dancing up and down with delight. "They're just lovely, Maida, and how sweet you were to think of it. But it was just like you."

"Now we must pack them," Maida said.

Four pairs of hands made light work of this. By nine o'clock all the boxes were filled and spread out temptingly in the show case. By a quarter past nine, three of the W.M.N.T.'s were in bed trying hard to get to sleep. But Maida stayed up. The boxes were not her only surprise.

After the others had gone, she and Granny worked for half an hour in the little shop.

The Saturday before Christmas dawned clear and fair. Rosie hallooed for Dicky and Arthur as she came out of doors at half-past seven and all three arrived at the shop together. Their faces took on such a comic look of surprise that Maida burst out laughing.

"But where did it all come from?" Rosie asked in bewilderment. "Maida, you slyboots, you must have done all this after we left."

Maida nodded.

But all Arthur and Dicky said was "Gee!" and "Jiminy crickets!" But Maida found these exclamatives quite as expressive as Rosie's hugs. And, indeed, she herself thought the place worthy of any degree of admiring enthusiasm.

The shop was so strung with garlands of Christmas green that it looked like a bower. Bunches of mistletoe and holly added their colors to the holiday cheer. Red Christmas bells hung everywhere.

"My goodness, I never passed such a day in my life," Maida said that night at dinner. She was telling it all to Granny, who had been away on mysterious business of her own. "It's been like a beehive here ever since eight o'clock this morning. If we'd each of us had an extra pair of hands at our knees and another at our waists, perhaps we could have begun to wait on all the people."

"Sure 'twas no more than you deserved for being such busy little bees," Granny approved.

"The only trouble was," Maida went on smilingly, "that they liked everything so much that they could not decide which they wanted most. Of course, the boys preferred Arthur's carvings and the girls Rosie's candy. But it was hard to say who liked Dicky's things the best."

Granny twinkled with delight. She had never told Maida, but she did not need to tell her, that Dicky was her favorite.

"And then the grown people who came, Granny! First Arthur's father on his way to work, then Mrs. Lathrop and Laura--they bought loads of things, and Mrs. Clark and Mrs. Doyle and even Mr. Flanagan bought a hockey-stick. He said," Maida dimpled with delight, "he said he bought it to use on Arthur and Rosie if they ever hooked jack again. Poor Miss Allison bought one of Arthur's 'cats'--what do you suppose for?"

Granny had no idea.

"To wind her wool on. Then Billy came at the last minute and bought everything that was left. And just think, Granny, there was a crowd of little boys and girls who had stood about watching all day without any money to spend and Billy divided among them all the things he bought. Guess how much money they made!"

Granny guessed three sums, and each time Maida said, triumphantly, "More!" At last Granny had to give it up.

"Arthur made five dollars and thirty cents. Dicky made three dollars and eighty-seven cents. Rosie made two dollars and seventy cents."

After dinner that night, Maida accompanied Rosie and Dicky on the Christmas-shopping expedition.

They went first to a big dry goods store with Dicky. They helped Dicky to pick out a fur collar for his mother from a counter marked conspicuously $2.98. The one they selected was of gray and brown fur. It was Maida's opinion that it was sable and chinchilla mixed.

Dicky's face shone with delight when at last he tucked the big round box safely under his arm. "Just think, I've been planning to do this for three years," he said, "and I never could have done it now if it hadn't been for you, Maida."

Next Dicky took the two little girls where they could buy razors. "The kind that goes like a lawn-mower," Rosie explained to the proprietor. The man stared hard before he showed them his stock. But he was very kind and explained to them exactly how the wonderful little machine worked.

Maida noticed that Rosie examined very carefully all the things displayed in windows and on counters. But nothing she saw seemed to satisfy her, for she did not buy.

"What is it, Rosie?" Maida asked after a while.

"I'm looking for something for my mother."

"I'll help you," Maida said. She took Rosie's hand, and, thus linked together, the two little girls discussed everything that they saw.

Suddenly, Rosie uttered a little cry of joy and stopped at a jeweler's window.

A tray with the label, "SOLID SILVER, $1," overflowed with little heart-shaped pendants.

"Mama'd love one of those," Rosie said. "She just loved things she could hang round her neck."

They went inside. "It's just what I want," Rosie declared. "But I wish I had a little silver chain for it. I can't afford one though," she concluded wistfully.

"Oh, I know what to do," Maida said. "Buy a piece of narrow black velvet ribbon. Once my father gave my mother a beautiful diamond heart. Mother used to wear it on a black velvet ribbon. Afterwards papa bought her a chain of diamonds. But she always liked the black velvet best and so did papa and so did I. Papa said it made her neck look whiter."

The other three children looked curiously at Maida when she said, "diamond heart." When she said, "string of diamonds," they looked at each other.

"Was that another of your dreams, Maida?" Rosie asked mischievously.

"Dreams!" Maida repeated, firing up. But before she could say anything that she would regret, the dimples came. "Perhaps it was a dream," she said prettily. "But if it was, then everything's a dream."

"I believe every word that Maida says," Dicky protested stoutly.

"I believe that Maida believes it," Arthur said with a smile.

They all stopped with Rosie while she bought the black velvet ribbon and strung the heart on it. She packed it neatly away in the glossy box in which the jeweler had done it up.

"If my mama doesn't come back to wear that heart, nobody else ever will," she said passionately. "Never--never--never--unless I have a little girl of my own some day."

"Your mother'll come back," Maida said.

CHAPTER XIV: CHRISTMAS HAPPENINGS

Maida was awakened early Christmas morning by a long, wild peal of the bell. Before she could collect her scattered wits, she heard Rosie's voice, "Merry Christmas! Merry Christmas! Merry Christmas! Oh, Granny, won't you please let me run upstairs and wake Maida? I've got something dreadfully important to tell her."

Maida heard Granny's bewildered "All roight, child," heard Rosie's rush through the living-room and then she bounded out of bed, prickling all over with excitement.

"Maida," Rosie called from the stairs, "wake up! I've something wonderful to tell you."

But Maida had guessed it.

"I know," she cried, as Rosie burst into the room. "Your mother's come home."

"My mother's come home," Rosie echoed.

The two little girls seized each other and hopped around the room in a mad dance, Maida chanting in a deep sing-song, "Your mother's come home!" and Rosie screaming at the top of her lungs, "My mother's come home!" After a few moments of this, they sank exhausted on the bed.

"Tell me all about it," Maida gasped. "Begin at the very beginning and don't leave anything out."

"Well, then," Rosie began, "I will. When I went to bed last night after leaving you, I got to thinking of my mother and pretty soon I was so sad that I nearly cried my eyes out. Well, after a long while I got to sleep and I guess I must have been very tired, for I didn't wake up the way I do generally of my own accord. Aunt Theresa had to wake me. She put on my best dress and did my hair this new way and even let me put cologne on. I couldn't think why, because I never dress up until afternoons. Once when I looked at her, I saw there were tears in her eyes and, oh, Maida, it made me feel something awful, for I thought she was going to tell me that my mother was dead. When I came downstairs, my father hugged me and kissed me and sat with me while I ate my breakfast. Oh, I was so afraid he was going to tell me that mother was dead! But he didn't! After awhile, he said, 'Your Christmas presents are all up in your mother's bedroom, Rosie.' So I skipped up there. My father and Aunt Theresa didn't come with me, but I noticed they stood downstairs and listened. I opened the door."

Rosie stopped for breath.

"Go on," Maida entreated; "oh, do hurry."

"Well, there, lying on the bed was my mother. Maida, I felt so queer that I couldn't move. My feet wouldn't walk---just like in a dream. My mother said, 'Come here, my precious little girl,' but it sounded as if it came from way, way, way off. And Maida *then* I could move. I ran across the room and hugged her and kissed her until I couldn't breathe. Then she said, 'I have a beautiful Christmas gift for you, little daughter,' and she pulled something over towards me that lay, all wrapped up, in a shawl on the bed. What do you think it was?"

"I don't know. Oh, tell me, Rosie!"

"Guess," Rosie insisted, her eyes dancing.

"Rosie, if you don't tell me this minute, I'll pinch you."

"It was a baby--a little baby brother."

"A baby! Oh, Rosie!"

The two little girls hopped about the room in another mad dance.

"Maida, he's the darlingest baby that ever was in the whole wide world! His name is Edward. He's only six weeks old and *he can smile*."

"Smile, Rosie?"

"He can--I saw him--and sneeze!"

"Sneeze, Rosie?"

"That's not all," said Rosie proudly. "He can wink his eyes and double up his fists--and--and--and a whole lot of things. There's no doubt that he's a remarkable baby. My mother says so. And pretty as--oh, he's prettier than any puppy I ever saw. He's a little too pink in the face and he hasn't much hair yet--there's a funny spot in the top of his head that goes up and down all the time that you have to be dreadfully careful about. But he certainly is the loveliest baby I ever saw. What do you think my mother let me do?"

"Oh, what?"

"She let me rock him for a moment. And I asked her if you could rock him some day and she said you could."

"Oh! oh!"

"And what else do you think she's going to let me do?"

"I can't guess. Oh, tell me quick, Rosie."

"She says she's going to let me give him his bath Saturdays and Sundays and wheel him out every day in his carriage."

"Rosie," Maida said impressively, "you ought to be the happiest little girl in the world. Think of having a baby brother for a Christmas present. You will let me wheel him sometimes, won't you?"

"Of course I will. I shall divide him exactly in half with you."

"Where has your mother been all this time?" Maida asked.

"Oh, she's been dreadfully sick in a hospital. She was sick after the baby came to her--so sick that she couldn't even take care of him. She said they were afraid she was going to die. But she's all right now. Father bought her for Christmas a beautiful, long, red-silk dress that's just to lie down in. She looks like a queen in it, and yet she looks like a little girl, too, for her hair is done in two braids. Her hair comes way down below her waist like your mother's hair. And when I gave her the little silver heart, she was so pleased with it. She put it right on and it looked sweet. She said she would much rather wear it on a black velvet ribbon than on a silver chain."

"Everything's come out all right, hasn't it?" Maida said with ecstasy.

"I guess it has. Now I must go. I want to be sure to be there when the baby wakes up. I asked my mother when you could see the baby, Maida, and she said to-morrow. I can't wait to show you its feet--you never did see such little toes in your life."

Exciting as this event was, it was as nothing to what followed.

Granny and Maida were still talking about Rosie's happiness when Billy Potter suddenly came marching through the shop and into the living-room.

"Merry Christmas! Merry Christmas! Merry Christmas!" they all said at once.

"Granny," Billy asked immediately, "if you could have your choice of all the Christmas gifts in the world, which one would you choose?"

An expression of bewilderment came into Granny's bright blue eyes.

"A Christmas gift, Misther Billy," she said in an uncertain tone; "I cudn't t'ink of a t'ing as long as Oi can't have me little Annie wid me."

Maida saw Billy's eyes snap and sparkle at the word Annie. She wondered what--Could it be possible that--She began to tremble.

"And so you'd choose your daughter, Granny?" Billy questioned.

"Choose my daughter. Av coorse Oi wud!" Granny stopped to stare in astonishment at Billy. "Oh, Misther Billy, if you cud only foind her!" She gazed imploringly at him. Billy continued to smile at her, his eyes all "skrinkled up." Granny jumped to her feet. She seized Billy's arm. "Oh, Misther Billy, you *have* found her," she quavered.

Billy nodded. "I've found her, Granny! I told you I would and I have. Now don't get excited. She's all right and you're all right and everything's all right. She'll be here just as soon as you're ready to see her."

For a moment Maida was afraid Granny was going to faint, for she dropped back into her chair and her eyes filled with tears. But at Billy's last words the old fire came back to her eyes, the color to her cheeks. "Oi want to see her at wance," she said with spirit.

"Listen," Billy said. "Last night I happened to fall into conversation with a young Irishman who had come to read the gas-meter in my house. I asked him where he came from. He said, 'Aldigarey, County Sligo.' I asked him if he knew Annie Flynn. 'Sure, didn't she marry my cousin? She lives--' Well, the short of it is that I went right over to see her, though it was late then. I found her a widow with two children. She nearly went crazy at the prospect of seeing her mother again, but we agreed that we must wait until morning. We planned--oh, come in, Annie," he called suddenly.

At his call, the shop door opened and shut. There was a rush of two pairs of feet through the shop. In the doorway appeared a young woman carrying a baby. Behind her came a little boy on crutches. Granny stood like a marble statue, staring. But Maida screamed.

Who do you suppose they were?

They were Mrs. Dore and Delia and Dicky.

"Oh, my mother!" Mrs. Dore said.

"My little Annie--my little girl," Granny murmured. The tears began to stream down her cheeks.

Followed kissings and huggings by the dozen. Followed questions and answers by the score.

"And to t'ink you've been living forninst us all this time," Granny said after the excitement had died down. She was sitting on the couch now, with Delia asleep in her lap, Mrs. Dore on one side and Dicky on the other. "And sure, me own hearrt was telling me the trut' all the toime did Oi but listhen to ut--for 'twas loving this foine little lad ivry minut av the day." She patted Dicky's head. "And me niver see-ing the baby that had me own name!" She cuddled Delia close. "OI'm the happiest woman in the whole woide wurrld this day."

It was arranged that the two families were to have Christmas dinner together. Dicky and Mrs. Dore hurried back for a few moments to bring their turkey to the feast.

"Granny, will you love me just the same now that you've got Dicky and Delia?" Maida said wistfully.

"Love you, my lamb? Sure, I'll love you all the more for 'twas t'rough you I met Misther Billy and t'rough Misther Billy I found me Annie. Ah, Misther Billy, 'tis the grand man you make for such a b'y that you are!"

"Yes, m'm," said Billy.

When Mrs. Dore returned, mother and daughter went to work on the dinner, while Billy and Maida and Dicky trimmed the tree. When the door opened, they caught bits of conversation, Granny's brogue growing thicker and thicker in her excitement, and Mrs. Dore relapsing, under its influence, into old-country speech. At such times, Maida noticed that Billy's eyes always "skrinkled up."

They were just putting the finishing touches to the tree when the window darkened suddenly. Maida looked up in surprise. And then, "Oh, my papa's come!" she screamed; "my papa's come to my Christmas tree after all!"

There is so much to tell about the Christmas tree that I don't know where to begin.

First of all came Laura and Harold. Mrs. Lathrop stopped with them for a moment to congratulate Mrs. Dore on finding her mother.

"Mrs. Lathrop, permit me to introduce my father, Mr. Westabrook," Maida said.

Mrs. Lathrop was very gracious. "The neighborhood have accepted your daughter as Mrs. Flynn's grandchild, Mr. Westabrook. But I guessed the truth from the first. I believed, however, that you wished the matter kept a secret and I have said nothing of it to anybody."

"I thank you, madam," said "Buffalo" Westabrook, bending on her one of his piercing scrutinies. "How ever the neighborhood accepted her, they have given her back her health. I can never be too grateful to them."

Came Rosie next with a, "Oh, Maida, if you could only have seen Edward when my mother bathed him to-night!" Came Arthur, came the Doyles, came the Clark twins with Betsy tagging at their heels. Last of all, to Maida's great delight, came Dr. Pierce.

Nobody was allowed to go into the shop where the tree stood until the last guest had arrived. But in spite of their impatience they had a gay half hour of waiting. Billy amused them with all kinds of games and tricks and jokes, and when he tired, Dr. Pierce, who soon became a great favorite, took them in hand.

Dr. Pierce sat, most of the evening, holding Betsy in his lap, listening to her funny baby chatter and roaring at her escapades. He took a great fancy to the Clark twins and made all manner of fun for the children by pretending that there was only one of them. "Goodness; how you do fly about!" he would say ruefully to Dorothy, "An instant ago you were standing close beside me," or "How can you be here on the couch," he would say to Mabel, "when there you are as plain as a pikestaff standing up in the corner?"

"What can you do about that leg, Eli?" Mr. Westabrook asked Dr. Pierce once when Dicky swung across the room.

"I've been thinking about that," Dr. Pierce answered briskly. "I guess Granny and Annie will have to let me take Dicky for a while. A few months in my hospital and he'll be jumping round here like a frog with the toothache."

"Oh, Dr. Pierce, do you think you can cure him?" Mrs. Dore asked, clasping her hands.

"Cure him!" Dr. Pierce answered with his jolliest laugh. "Of course we can.

He's not in half so bad a condition as Maida was when we straightened her out. Greinschmidt taught us a whole bag of tricks. Dicky could almost mend himself if he'd only stay still long enough. Look at Maida. Would you ever think she'd been much worse than Dicky?"

Everybody stared hard at Maida, seated on her father's knee, and she dimpled and blushed under the observation. She was dressed all in white--white ribbons, white sash, white socks and shoes, the softest, filmiest white cobweb dress. Her hair streamed loose--a cascade of delicate, clinging ringlets of the palest gold. Her big, gray eyes, soft with the happiness of the long day, reflected the firelight. Her cheeks had grown round as well as pink and dimpled.

She did not look sick.

"Oh, Dicky," she cried, "just think, you're going to be cured. Didn't I tell you when my father saw you, he'd fix it all right? My father's a magician!"

But Dicky could not answer. He was gulping furiously to keep back the tears of delight. But he smiled his radiant smile. Billy took everybody's attention away from him by turning an unexpected cartwheel in the middle of the floor.

Finally, Maida announced that it was time for the tree. They formed in line and marched into the shop to a tune that Billy thumped out of the silver-toned old spinet.

I wish you could have heard the things the children said.

The tree went close to the ceiling. Just above it, with arms outstretched, swung a beautiful Christmas angel. Hanging from it were all kinds of glittery, quivery, sparkly things in silver and gold. Festooned about it were strings of pop corn and cranberries. At every branch-tip glistened a long glass icicle. And the whole thing was ablaze with candles and veiled in a mist of gold and silver.

At the foot of the tree, groups of tiny figures in painted plaster told the whole Christmas Day story from the moment of the first sight of the star by the shepherds who watched their flocks to the arrival, at the manger, of the Wise Men, bearing gold, frankincense and myrrh.

Billy Potter disappeared for a moment and came in, presently, the most chubby and pink-faced and blue-eyed of Santa Clauses, in purple velvet trimmed with ermine, with long white hair and a long white beard.

I can't begin to name to you all the fruits of that magic tree. From Maida, there came to Rosie a big golden cage with a pair of canary birds, to Arthur a chest of wonderful tools, to Dicky a little bookcase full of beautiful books, to Laura a collection of sashes and ribbons, to Harold a long train of cars. For Molly, Betsy and the Clark twins came so many gifts that you could hardly count them all--dolls and dolls' wardrobes, tiny doll-houses and tinier doll-furniture. For Tim came a sled and bicycle.

To Maida came a wonderful set of paper boxes from Dicky, a long necklace of carved beads from Arthur, a beautiful blank-book, with all her candy recipes, beautifully written out, from Rosie, a warm little pair of knitted bed-shoes from Granny, a quaint, little, old-fashioned locket from Dr. Pierce--he said it had once belonged to another little sick girl who died.

From Billy came a book. Perhaps you can fancy how Maida jumped when she read "The Crystal Ball," by William Potter, on the cover. But I do not think you can imagine how pleased she looked when inside she read the printed dedication, "To Petronilla."

From her father came a beautiful miniature of her mother, painted on ivory. The children crowded about her to see the beautiful face of which Maida had told them so much. There was the mass of golden hair which she had described so proudly. There, too, was a heart-shaped pendant of diamonds, suspended from a black velvet ribbon tied close to the white throat.

The children looked at the picture. Then they looked at each other.

But Maida did not notice. She was watching eagerly while Dr. Pierce and Billy and her father opened her gifts to them.

She was afraid they would not understand. "They're to save time, you see, when you want to shave in a hurry," she explained.

"Maida," her father said gravely, "that is a very thoughtful gift. It's strange when you come to think of it, as busy a man as I am and with all the friends I have, nobody has ever thought to give me a safety razor."

"I don't know how I ever managed to get along without one," Dr. Pierce declared, his curls bobbing.

"As for me--I shall probably save about a third of my income in the future," Billy announced.

All three were so pleased that they laughed for a long time.

"I'm going to give you another Christmas present, Maida," Mr. Westabrook said suddenly, "I'm going to give us both one--a vacation. We're going to start for Europe, week after next."

"Oh, papa, papa, how lovely!" Maida said. "Shall we see Venice again? But how can I give up my little shop and my friends?"

"Maida going away!" the children exclaimed. "Oh, dear! oh, dear!" "But Mr. Westabrook, isn't Maida coming back again?" Rosie asked. "How I shall miss her!" Laura chimed in.

"Take my lamb away," Granny wailed. "Sure, she'll be tuk sick in those woild counthries! You'll have to take me wid you, Misther Westabrook--only--only--" She did not finish her sentence but her eyes went anxiously to her daughter's face.

"No, Granny, you're not to go," Mr. Westabrook said decisively; "You're to stay right here with your daughter and her children. You're all to run the shop and live over it. Maida's old enough and well enough to take care of herself now. And I think she'd better begin to take care of me as well. Don't you think so, Maida?"

"Of course I do, papa. If you need me, I want to."

"Mr. Westabrook," Molly broke into the conversation determinedly, "did you ever give Maida a pair of Shetland ponies?"

Mr. Westabrook bent on the Robin the most amused of his smiles.

"Yes," he said.

"And an automobile?" Tim asked.

Mr. Westabrook turned to the Bogle. "Yes," he said, a little puzzled.

"And did Maida's mother have a gold brush with her initials in diamonds on it?" Rosie asked.

Mr. Westabrook roared. "Yes," he said.

"And have you got twelve peacocks, two of them white?" Arthur asked.

"Yes."

"And has Maida a little theater of her own and a doll-house as big as a cottage?" Laura asked.

"Yes."

"And did she have a May-party last year that she invited over four hundred children to?" Harold asked.

"Yes."

"And did you give her her weight in silver dollars once?" Mabel asked.

"Yes."

"And a family of twenty dolls?" Dorothy asked.

"Yes, you shall see all these things when we come back," Mr. Westabrook promised.

"Then why did she run away?" Betsy asked solemnly.

Everybody laughed.

"I always said Maida was a princess in disguise," Dicky maintained, "and now I suppose she's going back and be a princess again."

"Dicky was the first friend I made, papa," Maida said, smiling at her first friend.

"But you'll come back some time, won't you, Maida?" Dicky begged.

"Yes, Dicky," Maida answered, "*I'll* come back."

Yes, Maida did come back. And what fun they all have, the Little Six in their private quarters, and the Big Six with their picnics, and their adventures with the Gypsies, is told in *Maida's Little House*.

The Codes Of Hammurabi And Moses
W. W. Davies

QTY

The discovery of the Hammurabi Code is one of the greatest achievements of archaeology, and is of paramount interest, not only to the student of the Bible, but also to all those interested in ancient history...

Religion   ISBN: *1-59462-338-4*   Pages:132

MSRP $12.95

The Theory of Moral Sentiments
Adam Smith

QTY

This work from 1749. contains original theories of conscience amd moral judgment and it is the foundation for systemof morals.

Philosophy ISBN: *1-59462-777-0*   Pages:536

MSRP $19.95

Jessica's First Prayer
Hesba Stretton

QTY

In a screened and secluded corner of one of the many railway-bridges which span the streets of London there could be seen a few years ago, from five o'clock every morning until half past eight, a tidily set-out coffee-stall, consisting of a trestle and board, upon which stood two large tin cans, with a small fire of charcoal burning under each so as to keep the coffee boiling during the early hours of the morning when the work-people were thronging into the city on their way to their daily toil...

Pages:84

Childrens   ISBN: *1-59462-373-2*   *MSRP $9.95*

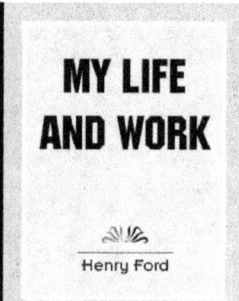

My Life and Work
Henry Ford

QTY

Henry Ford revolutionized the world with his implementation of mass production for the Model T automobile. Gain valuable business insight into his life and work with his own auto-biography... "We have only started on our development of our country we have not as yet, with all our talk of wonderful progress, done more than scratch the surface. The progress has been wonderful enough but..."

Pages:300

Biographies/   ISBN: *1-59462-198-5*   *MSRP $21.95*

The Art of Cross-Examination
Francis Wellman

I presume it is the experience of every author, after his first book is published upon an important subject, to be almost overwhelmed with a wealth of ideas and illustrations which could readily have been included in his book, and which to his own mind, at least, seem to make a second edition inevitable. Such certainly was the case with me; and when the first edition had reached its sixth impression in five months, I rejoiced to learn that it seemed to my publishers that the book had met with a sufficiently favorable reception to justify a second and considerably enlarged edition. ..

Reference   ISBN: *1-59462-647-2*   Pages:412   MSRP $19.95   QTY

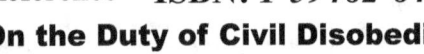

On the Duty of Civil Disobedience
Henry David Thoreau

Thoreau wrote his famous essay, On the Duty of Civil Disobedience, as a protest against an unjust but popular war and the immoral but popular institution of slave-owning. He did more than write—he declined to pay his taxes, and was hauled off to gaol in consequence. Who can say how much this refusal of his hastened the end of the war and of slavery ?

Law   ISBN: *1-59462-747-9*   Pages:48   MSRP $7.45   QTY

Dream Psychology Psychoanalysis for Beginners
Sigmund Freud

Sigmund Freud, born Sigismund Schlomo Freud (May 6, 1856 - September 23, 1939), was a Jewish-Austrian neurologist and psychiatrist who co-founded the psychoanalytic school of psychology. Freud is best known for his theories of the unconscious mind, especially involving the mechanism of repression; his redefinition of sexual desire as mobile and directed towards a wide variety of objects; and his therapeutic techniques, especially his understanding of transference in the therapeutic relationship and the presumed value of dreams as sources of insight into unconscious desires.

Psychology   ISBN: *1-59462-905-6*   Pages:196   MSRP $15.45   QTY

The Miracle of Right Thought
Orison Swett Marden

Believe with all of your heart that you will do what you were made to do. When the mind has once formed the habit of holding cheerful, happy, prosperous pictures, it will not be easy to form the opposite habit. It does not matter how improbable or how far away this realization may see, or how dark the prospects may be, if we visualize them as best we can, as vividly as possible, hold tenaciously to them and vigorously struggle to attain them, they will gradually become actualized, realized in the life. But a desire, a longing without endeavor, a yearning abandoned or held indifferently will vanish without realization.

Self Help   ISBN: *1-59462-644-8*   Pages:360   MSRP $25.45   QTY

The Rosicrucian Cosmo-Conception Mystic Christianity *by Max Heindel*   ISBN: *1-59462-188-8* **$38.95**
The Rosicrucian Cosmo-conception is not dogmatic, neither does it appeal to any other authority than the reason of the student. It is: not controversial, but is: sent forth in the, hope that it may help to clear...   New Age/Religion Pages 646

Abandonment To Divine Providence *by Jean-Pierre de Caussade*   ISBN: *1-59462-228-0* **$25.95**
"The Rev. Jean Pierre de Caussade was one of the most remarkable spiritual writers of the Society of Jesus in France in the 18th Century. His death took place at Toulouse in 1751. His works have gone through many editions and have been republished...   Inspirational/Religion Pages 400

Mental Chemistry *by Charles Haanel*   ISBN: *1-59462-192-6* **$23.95**
Mental Chemistry allows the change of material conditions by combining and appropriately utilizing the power of the mind. Much like applied chemistry creates something new and unique out of careful combinations of chemicals the mastery of mental chemistry...   New Age Pages 354

The Letters of Robert Browning and Elizabeth Barret Barrett 1845-1846 vol II   ISBN: *1-59462-193-4* **$35.95**
by Robert Browning and Elizabeth Barrett   Biographies Pages 596

Gleanings In Genesis (volume I) *by Arthur W. Pink*   ISBN: *1-59462-130-6* **$27.45**
Appropriately has Genesis been termed "the seed plot of the Bible" for in it we have, in germ form, almost all of the great doctrines which are afterwards fully developed in the books of Scripture which follow...   Religion/Inspirational Pages 420

The Master Key *by L. W. de Laurence*   ISBN: *1-59462-001-6* **$30.95**
In no branch of human knowledge has there been a more lively increase of the spirit of research during the past few years than in the study of Psychology, Concentration and Mental Discipline. The requests for authentic lessons in Thought Control, Mental Discipline and...   New Age/Business Pages 422

The Lesser Key Of Solomon Goetia *by L. W. de Laurence*   ISBN: *1-59462-092-X* **$9.95**
This translation of the first book of the "Lernegton" which is now for the first time made accessible to students of Talismanic Magic was done, after careful collation and edition, from numerous Ancient Manuscripts in Hebrew, Latin, and French...   New Age/Occult Pages 92

Rubaiyat Of Omar Khayyam *by Edward Fitzgerald*   ISBN:*1-59462-332-5* **$13.95**
Edward Fitzgerald, whom the world has already learned, in spite of his own efforts to remain within the shadow of anonymity, to look upon as one of the rarest poets of the century, was born at Bredfield, in Suffolk, on the 31st of March, 1809. He was the third son of John Purcell...   Music Pages 172

Ancient Law *by Henry Maine*   ISBN: *1-59462-128-4* **$29.95**
The chief object of the following pages is to indicate some of the earliest ideas of mankind, as they are reflected in Ancient Law, and to point out the relation of those ideas to modern thought.   Religion/History Pages 452

Far-Away Stories *by William J. Locke*   ISBN: *1-59462-129-2* **$19.45**
"Good wine needs no bush, but a collection of mixed vintages does. And this book is just such a collection. Some of the stories I do not want to remain buried for ever in the museum files of dead magazine-numbers an author's not unpardonable vanity..."   Fiction Pages 272

Life of David Crockett *by David Crockett*   ISBN: *1-59462-250-7* **$27.45**
"Colonel David Crockett was one of the most remarkable men of the times in which he lived. Born in humble life, but gifted with a strong will, an indomitable courage, and unremitting perseverance...   Biographies/New Age Pages 424

Lip-Reading *by Edward Nitchie*   ISBN: *1-59462-206-X* **$25.95**
Edward B. Nitchie, founder of the New York School for the Hard of Hearing, now the Nitchie School of Lip-Reading, Inc, wrote "LIP-READING Principles and Practice". The development and perfecting of this meritorious work on lip-reading was an undertaking...   How-to Pages 400

A Handbook of Suggestive Therapeutics, Applied Hypnotism, Psychic Science   ISBN: *1-59462-214-0* **$24.95**
by Henry Munro   Health/New Age/Health/Self-help Pages 376

A Doll's House: and Two Other Plays *by Henrik Ibsen*   ISBN: *1-59462-112-8* **$19.95**
Henrik Ibsen created this classic when in revolutionary 1848 Rome. Introducing some striking concepts in playwriting for the realist genre, this play has been studied the world over.   Fiction/Classics/Plays 308

The Light of Asia *by sir Edwin Arnold*   ISBN: *1-59462-204-3* **$13.95**
In this poetic masterpiece, Edwin Arnold describes the life and teachings of Buddha. The man who was to become known as Buddha to the world was born as Prince Gautama of India but he rejected the worldly riches and abandoned the reigns of power when...   Religion/History/Biographies Pages 170

The Complete Works of Guy de Maupassant *by Guy de Maupassant*   ISBN: *1-59462-157-8* **$16.95**
"For days and days, nights and nights, I had dreamed of that first kiss which was to consecrate our engagement, and I knew not on what spot I should put my lips..."   Fiction/Classics Pages 240

The Art of Cross-Examination *by Francis L. Wellman*   ISBN: *1-59462-309-0* **$26.95**
Written by a renowned trial lawyer, Wellman imparts his experience and uses case studies to explain how to use psychology to extract desired information through questioning.   How-to/Science/Reference Pages 408

Answered or Unanswered? *by Louisa Vaughan*   ISBN: *1-59462-248-5* **$10.95**
Miracles of Faith in China   Religion Pages 112

The Edinburgh Lectures on Mental Science (1909) *by Thomas*   ISBN: *1-59462-008-3* **$11.95**
This book contains the substance of a course of lectures recently given by the writer in the Queen Street Hall, Edinburgh. Its purpose is to indicate the Natural Principles governing the relation between Mental Action and Material Conditions...   New Age/Psychology Pages 148

Ayesha *by H. Rider Haggard*   ISBN: *1-59462-301-5* **$24.95**
Verily and indeed it is the unexpected that happens! Probably if there was one person upon the earth from whom the Editor of this, and of a certain previous history, did not expect to hear again...   Classics Pages 380

Ayala's Angel *by Anthony Trollope*   ISBN: *1-59462-352-X* **$29.95**
The two girls were both pretty, but Lucy who was twenty-one who supposed to be simple and comparatively unattractive, whereas Ayala was credited, as her Bombwhat romantic name might show, with poetic charm and a taste for romance. Ayala when her father died was nineteen...   Fiction Pages 484

The American Commonwealth *by James Bryce*   ISBN: *1-59462-286-8* **$34.45**
An interpretation of American democratic political theory. It examines political mechanics and society from the perspective of Scotsman James Bryce   Politics Pages 572

Stories of the Pilgrims *by Margaret P. Pumphrey*   ISBN: *1-59462-116-0* **$17.95**
This book explores pilgrims religious oppression in England as well as their escape to Holland and eventual crossing to America on the Mayflower, and their early days in New England...   History Pages 268

QTY

The Fasting Cure *by Sinclair Upton* ISBN: *1-59462-222-1* **$13.95**
In the Cosmopolitan Magazine for May, 1910, and in the Contemporary Review (London) for April, 1910, I published an article dealing with my experiences in fasting. I have written a great many magazine articles, but never one which attracted so much attention... New Age/Self Help/Health Pages 164 ☐

Hebrew Astrology *by Sepharial* ISBN: *1-59462-308-2* **$13.45**
In these days of advanced thinking it is a matter of common observation that we have left many of the old landmarks behind and that we are now pressing forward to greater heights and to a wider horizon than that which represented the mind-content of our progenitors... Astrology Pages 144 ☐

Thought Vibration or The Law of Attraction in the Thought World ISBN: *1-59462-127-6* **$12.95**
by William Walker Atkinson Psychology/Religion Pages 144 ☐

Optimism *by Helen Keller* ISBN: *1-59462-108-X* **$15.95**
Helen Keller was blind, deaf, and mute since 19 months old, yet famously learned how to overcome these handicaps, communicate with the world, and spread her lectures promoting optimism. An inspiring read for everyone... Biographies/Inspirational Pages 84 ☐

Sara Crewe *by Frances Burnett* ISBN: *1-59462-360-0* **$9.45**
In the first place, Miss Minchin lived in London. Her home was a large, dull, tall one, in a large, dull square, where all the houses were alike, and all the sparrows were alike, and where all the door-knockers made the same heavy sound... Childrens/Classic Pages 88 ☐

The Autobiography of Benjamin Franklin *by Benjamin Franklin* ISBN: *1-59462-135-7* **$24.95**
The Autobiography of Benjamin Franklin has probably been more extensively read than any other American historical work, and no other book of its kind has had such ups and downs of fortune. Franklin lived for many years in England, where he was agent... Biographies/History Pages 332 ☐

Name	
Email	
Telephone	
Address	
City, State ZIP	

☐ **Credit Card**   ☐ **Check / Money Order**

Credit Card Number	
Expiration Date	
Signature	

Please Mail to: Book Jungle
PO Box 2226
Champaign, IL 61825
or Fax to: 630-214-0564

ORDERING INFORMATION

web*: www.bookjungle.com*
email*: sales@bookjungle.com*
fax*: 630-214-0564*
mail*: Book Jungle PO Box 2226 Champaign, IL 61825*
or PayPal *to sales@bookjungle.com*

Please contact us for bulk discounts

DIRECT-ORDER TERMS

**20% Discount if You Order
Two or More Books**
Free Domestic Shipping!
Accepted: Master Card, Visa,
Discover, American Express

www.ingramcontent.com/pod-product-compliance
Lightning Source LLC
Chambersburg PA
CBHW080824020726
47501CB00009B/2412